Run With the Hunted
By Jennifer R. Donohue

Run with the Hunted © 2018 by Jennifer R. Donohue

ISBN: 978-1-945548-04-8

For Jim

Chapter One

Bits called our latest meeting when she sniffed out the job, but I chose the location: one of our local museums, free on Wednesdays. I arrive after a predictably disappointing date, removing that man's contact from my phone, and I find Bits sitting on a bench, a bouquet of snack bags peeking from her cargo pocket. It's possible she subsists entirely on vending machine food; I hesitate to ask.

"Hey Bristol. Their beverage restock isn't until tomorrow," she says when I sit next to her, smoothing my skirt. "I got one of those fizzy things you like so much, to try it, but it was the last one. You don't mind, do you?"

"That you took the last one, or that you opened a drink you're passing along to me?" I ask with a laugh.

"Whichever." Bits's existence is one of the perpetual slouch and shrug.

"No, I don't mind. I came from a wine tasting."

"Fancy. Was he second date material?"

"He was not. He had money, but not enough that it was sufficient substitute for things like charm or morals."

"Morals," Bits repeats, like it's funny.

"Yes, morals. He had no sense of how people ought to be treated." She nods, looking at the painting in front of us, a large, drab rendering of a fox hunt. I get the sense she already knows who my date was, and is unsurprised by the result.

Dolly walks in. If we are not opposites, then we are something close to it. I've taken care to cultivate my appearance, for the entrance I make. To ensure my makeup, my posture, my hair, are all done just so, I've pored over style guides and purchased pirated online courses from finishing schools.

When Dolly enters a room, people notice, but in a different way. In a checking for security, checking exits kind of way. Dolly smiles easily, big and brash and daring you to fuck with her. Dolly walks in like she owns the place, or will own the place, whether you like it or not, and her clothing is always off by at least a slight degree. Waistband slung too low, boots too heavy, t-shirt too tight.

"Y'all like the painting?" Dolly asks, at full volume and with broadened on-purpose Southern drawl, drawing short glances and slight frowns from the other museum goers.

I cross the room to Dolly and link arms with her, smiling serenely. "You're making a scene."

"Aw, fuck 'em," Dolly says, though she lowers her voice. "You want to stay here or get something to eat?"

"We could eat at the museum restaurant." I do not care to tramp through the city to whatever food truck these two would prefer to frequent.

"Have you seen those prices?" Bits asks. "I could pay rent for a month with what they're charging for salmon."

"Salmon has become rather dear."

"Not too dear, they farm 'em in all those rice fields they got in California now. It's just artificial inflation."

"Bits, I'll buy your lunch. You will not sit at a table with us eating whatever you have squirreled away in your pockets, it's far too much."

Bits shrugs. "If you say so."

We file through the museum restaurant. I get the salad bar, and Dolly and Bits order from the holo menu. We sit down to wait.

The silverware is surprisingly heavy, like picking up a handgun for the first time. I grind some pepper on my salad and fork the lettuce around to mix the dressing. Soon, Dolly's salmon and Bits's lasagna are brought to the table. "So what do we have?" I ask. Bits reaches for her pocket and I shake my head. "Just tell us, no holos here."

"An independent dealer, with legit certificates, is bringing a bajillion carats of diamonds into town for a private showing."

"By a bajillion karats, do you mean a very large diamond, or many small ones?"

"A combination, I think. A lot of high brilliance but small gems, but a couple of big ones too. Including one of those mythic 'biggest blue diamond ever found in Shangri-la' or whatever stones."

"If it's blue, it's probably Australian or South African," I say. "Go on."

"Invitations have been sent out to some upper crusty people. Some jewelers and some private collectors. An ostrich baron. An opera singer."

"An ostrich baron?" Dolly hoots, and I shoot her a narrow-eyed look. "Sorry, it's just we've been waiting so long for the ostrich boom to happen."

"Who's we?" I ask.

"The royal we. The world."

I look at her blankly and Bits takes pity on me. "Ostriches are more green than cattle. They need less land and have a smaller carbon footprint, so somebody could do double duty raising cheap lean meat and selling their allowance of carbon certificates."

"Okay, I'll ask. Why does everybody but me know about the market demands and environmental significance of ostriches?"

"We're just more practical than you, Bristles."

"Of course." I will not comment on the unwanted nickname; it never does any good. We eat in silence until the holographic check pops up. I tap my meal and Bits's to pay. "What kind of security do they maintain?"

"The hotel security is what you'd expect, cameras and rent-a-cops with walkies. They're not going to engage, just call police. Police response to that property is inside five minutes. They have panic buttons at the front desk, and in the security office."

"And what's their network security like?"

"They have guest wireless, but all the staff stuff, cameras and reservations, is hardwired. Server is in the basement. Staff is the weak link, they prop doors to go outside and smoke all the time."

"So we need security suppressed, we need to get in that room, and we need at least two exit strategies, yes?" I finish my salad, push the bowl to the side.

"Havin' a buyer lined up might be nice," Dolly says.

I wave my hand dismissively. "I might know somebody."

"These diamonds will all have identifiers," Bits says. "Little laser etchings. Sometimes it's a barcode, sometimes a serial number."

"Once they're in a setting, nobody will ever care to check that," I say. "Or, if it is checked, years down the line when somebody gets their engagement ring cleaned or something, it isn't our problem."

"That big blue one, somebody'll recognize." Dolly pushes her own empty plate aside.

"Maybe we should ransom it," I say with a wicked smile.

"I don't want the risk of that. Too many points of contact gives them that much more intel to find us."

"Nobody's ever even gonna see you, Itsy-Bitsy," Dolly says. "You'll what, sneak in that propped door, set yourself up in a towel closet, and tap into their datastream?"

"Yeah, probably," Bits says.

"Really, we shouldn't get our hearts set on a plan until we know more about the hotel, and the meeting," I say. "And how one gets invitations."

"I'm pretty sure their guest list is set."

"*Anyway.*" Dolly rolls her eyes. "Broad strokes. You get the cameras handled, Bits, then Bristol and I make our way up to the room. We bypass the locks, we get the rocks in the bag, then we split."

"Split how?" I prompt.

"Bits can commandeer the elevators, make it so we can ride one straight to the basement. There's all kinds of fire doors in a place like that, and lots of alleys beyond. Won't take long to lose anybody in the city, and then regroup."

I nod. "Okay for a plan A. Plan B?"

"I trip the alarm systems, and everybody in the hotel empties out until emergency personnel clear it. You two can walk right out the front door and into a cab or something, and I can go out the way I came. We'll be long gone before things clear up."

"Do you ever long for a personal helicopter?" I muse, pulling up the holo menu and browsing the drinks idly. I don't want more wine. Perhaps something wicked like a milkshake? But no.

"Riot gear for this, yeah?" We all have riot gear, Dolly's name for it, though it is not my preference. Ripstop cargo pants with Kevlar in the knees and shins, turtlescale longsleeved shirts—thank you NASA for that particular technology—steel shank combat boots. Jackets or utility vests optional. Assorted face masks, with rebreathers and otherwise.

"The riot gear should suffice," I sigh. "Though I *do* think I'm going to see if I can secure myself an actual invitation to the event, in which case I'll wear one of my lined dresses."

"You won't want to take all those stairs in your heels," Bits says.

"I practically live in heels, hotel stairs won't bother me in the slightest."

"If you say so." Bits drums her fingertips on the table. "We have a shopping list?"

"Other than an invitation, I'm sure I have everything I need. Dolly?"

"Might need to top off my ammo stores, but that doesn't really concern you two. What are we thinking for transport, helicopter aside?"

"The lowest profile possible, it's the one time I don't want attention. Investigate the nearby side streets and alleyways for potential getaway vehicles?"

"Already covered," Bits says.

"Perfect! We arrive separately, do our parts, and depending on how the grab strategy works out, we leave on foot to meet the car, or a well timed cab. We won't be recognizable, and it isn't as though even that many stones will be too bulky to divvy up and carry easily. Simple."

"If you wanna borrow trouble, calling a job simple is the way to do it." Dolly pays for her meal. "Let's get out of here, all this culture makes me itch."

"Perhaps you should see a doctor."

Chapter Two

If you can imagine such a thing, I do have matters on my mind other than diamond heists. My dear friend Jules is flying in from Europe to review a show, and will be available for only a handful of nights. It simply will not do to let the occasion slide, so I find myself planning a party. It won't be extravagant; just wine and cheese and some manner of dessert, perhaps petit fours.

As luck would have it, while I am feeling out prospective diamond buyers, I learn that my dear friend Marquis in fact has an invitation to the showing in question. Marquis has a penchant for saying yes to every invitation, and an inability to be in two places at once, and I video call them directly. "Darling."

"It has been far too long," they say, getting their cufflinks into place. "What have you been up to, Bristol?"

"Such dreadfully boring pursuits, I won't even drag them all out before you. Though I will be having a tiny party in the next week or so. Perhaps you'd like to attend?"

"That does sound delightful." Marquis finishes their cuffs, looking at the screen intently. "I'm on my way to a show now, though. I haven't got much time to talk. Can I call you later? Or we can have coffee tomorrow?"

"Of course, I don't want to keep you."

"Good. I'll come around at ten for you. We'll go to the place beneath the aquarium, that we might have coffee and croissants in the presence of giants."

"In the presence of giants?"

"Well *a* giant. That old blind whale that I'm sure they just can't release anywhere, and so instead it looms endlessly over the cafe."

"Oh the poor thing, if we must. At ten, then." Marquis makes a kissy face and ends the call.

The next morning, I select my outfit with the care necessary to make it look thrown together. Polished cognac leather boots, knee high over black leggings, with a tunic length charcoal sweater and a large leather handbag, which complements the boots without matching them exactly. No diamonds in my jewelry, I don't have very many anyway, and I pull my hair back in a sort of messy bun.

"You're a vision," Marquis says, as we kiss cheeks.

"Oh please. My wardrobe doesn't begin to approach yours, for one." Marquis is wearing another of their signature tailored shirts, a different set of cufflinks, very dark washed skinny jean, and boots as well, but the kind designed to remain artfully untied instead of the slovenly way Dolly's sometimes do.

"One day, my dear, I'll get you on a runway," Marquis says.

"I'm not tall enough," I laugh, and Marquis hands me into the back seat of their car to cross town. Their driver wears a cap like the olden days, and thin leather driving gloves, and behaves as though he never hears a word we say. Sometimes it is a fun game to try and see if we can get a reaction from him, but this isn't the current mood. "You've been working too hard," I say.

"I am. It's so hard to get reliable help at the gallery. Are you sure you won't come work for me?"

"Oh, we would never be able to stay friends this way if I did. So I'm sorry, no. Though there must be some other way I can help." We arrive at the coffee shop, and the whale tank is a monstrosity. I wonder whatever possessed them to build it in the first place. We order our coffees and pastries and settle into a cozy corner table.

"This is more business than pleasure, then," Marquis says, sipping their tall and elaborate coffee drink, resplendent with syrups and a fluffy expanse of foamed milk.

"I do think the two can exist side by side," I say, wringing out the lemon slice into my espresso.

"Of course you do, and really, you aren't entirely wrong." Marquis blows on the foam on top of their drink, causing a tiny sinkhole. "But I know what type of business you do."

"Well yes. I hold you in the utmost of confidences; a girl can't keep secrets from her closest friends, it would simply drive me mad." I glance up at the whale, its inexorable pace. It reminds me of a dream I'd had in the midst of some childhood fever, where everything was moving but at a sliding freefall, not as quickly as it should be, but inevitable as death. Perhaps this was the wrong place to have come with Marquis at all, much less to discuss a successful diamond grab.

"Shall I guess what you want out of this?"

"If you'd like to make a game of it. I could just tell you."

Marquis smiles slyly. "No, I think I have it. Does it have to do with what else might be a girl's best friend?"

"It does." The whale flicks a fin.

"How did you know I'd get an invite?"

"It would be very crass for me to reveal my secrets."

"Of course." We sip our drinks in companionable silence. "You realize I can't be involved, so if you take my invitation, you yourself have to remain the picture of innocence."

"Of course. Putting you in danger is the last thing I want. And really, it'll be safer for my people if somebody is on the inside, counting noses and assessing threats."

"You just have an aversion to cargo pants." Marquis shakes their head, smiling.

"I haven't the hips for them, though I did just buy the most darling pair of black velvet combat boots."

"You'll have my invitation," Marquis says. "And yes, it is a help. That social obligation was a dreadful sword of Damocles, and I know you can act in my interests, which in this case is just making polite conversation and drinking bubbly. I had no intention of making any purchases."

"Yes, I'll make sure your reputation remains spotless. Thank you, Marquis."

"You're welcome, my dear." Marquis reaches over and peels a piece off of my croissant. "I shall notify the hosts you'll be taking my place, and send my invitation over to you."

"That sounds perfect." I look up; the whale has moved on to another portion of the tank and I can only see a swimmy white slice of the overcast sky up through the water. It's less of a relief than I thought it would be.

Of course, Dolly and Bits will be miffed that I've gone ahead and changed the plan, but I did warn them. Once Marquis and I leave each other, I send them requests to meet up after dark at a diner near to where Dolly may or may not be based. The sooner I might inform them, the better, that they might have time to air their frustrations before the job is at hand.

I DRAW LOOKS IN THE diner; it is a more working class establishment than I am used to and I seem misplaced. Only a few other people are here, some coffee-drinking political arguers at the counter, an older couple having the dinner special. I sit at a window booth with my thick ceramic mug of coffee and wait for the girls, who arrive together. I wonder if they spend much recreational time together, or if they were just engaged in all of their tiresome equipment checks. They slide into the booth across from me and the waitress appears with more coffee.

"So what's the new plan?" Dolly asks, sighing as she leans back with her arms folded.

"You can come up through a side door, I'll have already sabotaged the door lock and assessed private security, you burst in and pull the holdup."

"So you'll drink and hobnob with the rich folks while Bits and me do the work," Dolly says flatly.

I sigh slightly, trying not to think about the nameless stickiness of the floor beneath the soles of my boots. "I'll be keeping business relations smooth for Marquis, making sure the diamonds are what we thought they were and thus worth taking. I'm at most risk here, in that I'll be spending lots of time with both our victims and the authorities once they arrive. But by all means, Dolly, tell me again how your five minutes of shock and awe is far more risky and difficult than my role."

"If it's that bad, why offer to do it?" Bits asks. She's been putting one packet of sweetener after the other into her coffee, stirring, sampling it.

"It's worth the risk. I can handle it. And it's the way that makes Marquis seem blameless in this, and that's important to me."

"None of the rest of us were interested in involving Marquis," Dolly says. "Never even told us you were gonna."

"I'm sure I mentioned something to the effect." The waitress comes by with the coffee pot to top us all off, and Bits orders a stack of pancakes, Dolly some kind of hash.

"The circles you talk, you could've mentioned a pleasure cruise to Venus and we'd never question you. It takes its toll." She grins. She's still angry, but I've already won, of course.

"I didn't mean to make decisions without you and get anybody upset. It'll be alright, you'll see. And I have a line on a buyer as well. Bits, I've sent you the information."

"Received." She pauses a moment, looking at something in AR. "So are we set *now*?"

"Yes. We have a magnificent plan, cross my heart I will change nothing."

"If you say so," Dolly grumbles. "Though I swear, Bristles, if we agree to this and you call us tomorrow with another idea..."

"I won't, Dolly. Pinky swear." I smile and hold out my hand, and Dolly pushes it away.

"Sure, whatever. Bits, you're okay with this?"

"It's probably the best plan we've come up with. And by we I mean Bristol. I didn't have a better plan. It keeps us all safe, more or less, with minimal exposure. Dolly, do you even have nonlethal..."

"Yeah, I have a beanbag shotgun, and there's these weird compression gel things they have for handguns that I haven't tried yet. The magazines come preloaded. I'm surprised you even know about them, Bristol."

"I know about any number of things." I sip my coffee and stifle my grimace.

Chapter Three

I do not receive Marquis' invitation; the diamond sellers send me a fresh one, on actual paper with a digital chip in it which both verifies my currently claimed identity and plays a holographic display of the diamonds which will be offered for sale. I spend some time playing with the holograph, making the diamonds larger and smaller. The blue one really is breathtaking. And selling the lot, even at a cut black market rate, will be a tidy sum.

I dress with particular care, making sure the bionic earbuds are set properly, that there are no hitches in the turtlescale armor running like tulle through my just-understated-enough party dress. I have yet to be shot, and hope to continue that trend, though I would rather be protected than not. My stockings are not bullet or stab proof, but they can resist heat, flame, and chemicals. One heel sheaths a ceramic blade.

My gold jewelry was not my mother's, nor my grandmother's before her, though that's what I tell people about my simple pendant and chain, and dangling drop earrings. It's a pretty fiction. Where I come from, we have no heirlooms, no family touchstones.

I sweep my hair into a French twist. The hairpin has a tiny vial of pepper spray in the handle, and will separate into another blade if need be. I do hope there is no need.

I am not a gunner like Dolly, and I'm not an expert in knife fighting, but I have my tricks. Playing upon the unexpected nature of a sudden offense is a large part of my arsenal; nobody expects a girl like me to be able to fight back.

My purse contains the usual things, wallet with physical ID, a secondary phone to use for show, a variety of lipsticks, one of which is an explosive gel, my favorite way to manage small difficulties like door locks. My main phone is a slim and chic bracelet that Bits finagled for me, surrounded and camouflaged by other thin golden charm bracelets.

I stop at the hotel front desk with my thick paper invitation. The clerk scans the embedded microchip and directs me to the proper elevator. Once I'm alone again, Bits's whispery voice comes through my earbud. "Swanky. This must be where the mayor comes with his flings. Security is all contained with the building. The lines out are billing, emergency, and regular telecommunications."

"What does that mean for us?" I ask as I fix my lipstick in the elevator's mirrored wall.

"Nothing yet. Might make it easier to keep security away from you and Dolly. Well. Dolly. Or it might make it so if she gets caught—if *we* get caught—they can do whatever they want without the police ever knowing."

"Well." I don't have much to say to that.

"Right?" Bits laughs wryly. "So don't get us caught, okay?"

"I'll do my very best." I uncap the gel stick and work it into a wad. When the elevator reaches my floor it slides open with a pleasant tone, as though one had just climbed some serene mountain and hammered the gong at the top. The suite is at the entire opposite end of the hallway, the fire door halfway between the two.

I knock, and a very large man in a nice suit opens the door. The walls behind him are entirely glass, looking out over the city lights strewn like diamonds across the landscape. The other invitees are in various stages of being seated in a sunken living room, and I can smell the leather of the furniture from the doorway. "Oh, I do hope I'm not too late," I say in a very slight fluster, as though I've been rushing, and I make a show of juggling my purse and lipsticks about, pressing the gel into the doorjamb when that large man looks away in exasperation. "I didn't mean to keep anybody waiting."

The diamond seller is easy enough to pick out, classic briefcase cuffed to his left wrist. Also among the attendees are a trio of women so liberally draped in diamonds I can't imagine they're here to buy anything, and a handful of men in nondescript suits. It's simply the trend of men's clothing; the more expensive it is, the more plain it becomes. I do wonder if the ostrich rancher is attending, and which one he is. It seems gauche to ask; I shall have to consider shoes closely.

"Please, have a seat. May I bring you refreshment?" The barman is the right level of welcoming and attentive. Also armed. With a slight thrill, fear or excitement, I wonder if this diamond party is more than we had considered. But it is also the most appealing job we've had in a very long time.

"It might be wicked of me, but I would like some of that champagne, if somebody would share it with me. I'd hate to have a bottle opened only on my account."

"What are you celebrating?" one of the men asks. He's the right type, not too young, not yet old enough to start graying.

"Do I need to celebrate anything in particular? There's this lovely gathering, our beautiful view..." I turn to gesture, as the champagne cork is popped, and recognize one of the women from a gallery opening, I think. One of the other men is the opera singer. These are people with the means to buy diamonds, surely, though not the inclination.

"We may as well get on with it," one of the women says, turning to the man with the briefcase. She has no refreshments, and her shoes are a bit too serviceable to be partywear.

The man who'd spoken to me accepted a champagne flute, and I take my own and perch on the arm of his chair. He is *very* handsome, dashing and dark-featured like the old movies. "Just spectating, or are you a buyer?" he asks in a low voice as the man with the briefcase prepares the table.

"Oh just spectating," I say with a smile.

"Same. I heard the blue one was impressive, but those holos were on another level." He looks out of his element, and I try to picture what his element is. Yacht club? Board room? Neither seem to quite match.

"It was a very nice touch," I say.

"Will," he says, offering his hand.

"Chelsea." I clasp his hand in the barest of shakes, and he takes the invitation correctly, brushing the back of my hand with his lips. I smile and ignore Bits's snickering in my ears. Chelsea isn't my name any more than Bristol is, of course, but it's the fake identity I inhabit when dealing with people in legitimate business. Any of my accounts for the future are in another name entirely, offshore and DNA locked.

"I don't think I've seen you around," he says, and the corner of his mouth twitches. He's used to having better lines, I think.

"No, this was a rare opportunity for me." I lean in a little closer to him, catch the whiff of clean and oceanic aftershave from his neck and jaw. "This isn't one of those dreadful bidding situations, is it?" I ask, sotto voce.

"No, this is the showing. Any actual money will exchange hands at a later date."

"There's only so many ways to arrange shiny rocks on black velvet," the older woman snaps. "Any day now Richard."

"Yes, Mrs. Carter," Richard of the now no longer hand-cuffed briefcase says. "Ladies and gentlemen, if you would step over here into the better light, so you can view the color and clarity of the stones. These here, the ones set in the briefcase, are the master stones against which you may check the clear ones." Then, with a small amount of ceremony which draws a derisive sniff from Mrs. Carter, he pulls the blue diamond from another compartment in the briefcase and lays it slightly apart. "With colored stones, as I'm sure you know, that isn't how the grading works. But you've already received the holographic information regarding the authenticity and grading of this particular stone."

Mrs. Carter, that overachiever, is already reaching for the blue stone. Her clothing is so gaudy it can only be designer, though perhaps she isn't dressing in a way that best shows her qualities.

"And the provenance of all of these gems are legitimate?" One of the other men asks. He fiddles with an e cigarette, as though he isn't sure if anybody would object to his using it.

"There are varying levels of legitimate, Nathan," Mrs. Carter says dismissively. I get the sense this Mrs. Carter intends to purchase the lot, and simply arranged this get together for the theater of it.

"Some more savory than others," he says.

"Do you really want to bring up blood diamonds here and now?" she asks.

"I suppose not." He puts the e cigarette back into its little leather case and tucks it inside his jacket pocket.

In my earbud, Bits says "Sorry, Dolly's almost there."

"Thank you," I say, both to answer Bits and to accept another glass of bubbly. The guardsman is to the side of the door, and at a glance seems mildly bored and mostly centered on Richard the diamond seller, which is curious. Perhaps if I could place Richard's accent, or Mrs. Carter's, it would be clearer to me. "Won't you have anything?" I call lightly. "It's hard to enjoy champagne with people who aren't imbibing. You're not lonely over there, by the door?"

"No, miss," he answers shortly. "No drinking on the job."

"Right," I say, both because it makes sense and because he sits to the right of the door.

"Thanks," Dolly says, finally online with the rest of us. "There are some interesting cars in the lot. Fancy ones of course, but I swear, at least one is unmarked government, which probably means it's more like three."

I look around the room again. That could be another explanation for Mrs. Carter; she's a spy, and every little bit of her appearance has been cultivated for the reactions received. Appearances are very important, and realities are hard to discern, socially, virtually. It occurs to me that my close companion's tie pin looks rather like one of Bit's littlest cameras, and from my vantage, I can see the curve his earbud. But if this is some manner of deeply shadowed government thing... I set my champagne glass down and try to formulate how to make my exit, how to say the magic words which will pull the plug on this job—and then comes the hushed noise which means the gel in the doorjamb has received its little remote electrical charge. Nobody in the room seems to register the noise.

Mrs. Carter is once again examining the blue diamond. The men have moved away a bit, so Will and I have a place at the table to look at the smaller, clear stones. They are remarkable, and I wistfully poke a finger at their bright hard glitter. They would make glorious jewelry in single settings or in an extravagant cascade across a woman's bared clavicle. They will more than likely live in the dark, in black velvet boxes locked away in a bank vault, or a hidden wall safe behind some country manor style paintings in their tiresome gilt frames.

And the blue one... I lean forward a little to get a better look. It's hard to even describe the color. Like the sky after a hard rain, thinned out and scrubbed clean. Mrs. Carter gives me a warning look and I give her an innocent eyed, polite smile before turning to Will. I don't get a chance to speak, though, as the door kicks in at that moment, striking the wall behind it.

Even prepared to see Dolly in her riot gear, it is a startling moment, and I jump and gasp with the rest of them, reflexively clutching at Will's sleeve. Dolly is swiftly in the room, sweeping it with her shotgun. She circles hard to the side when the door slams shut, the guard gaining his feet, knocking his chair over. "On the ground," Dolly says. She isn't yelling, but her gas mask dehumanizes her voice. "Keep your hands clear." The guard doesn't look at Dolly, he looks at Mrs. Carter, who is frozen with such a look of hate and disgust on her face that I can only study her for a moment. She seems affronted, not frightened.

Nobody moves for a very long time, and I wonder if I'll have to step in, but then Dolly racks her shotgun. Mrs. Carter nods. "Do what they say," she says, glaring daggers. The guard sinks to his knees, then lowers his front to the floor. She stares at the barman until he does so as well.

"Start bagging up the merchandise," Dolly barks at Richard, throwing a black duffle bag on the floor.

"It'll be okay," Will murmurs, and I wonder for a mad moment who he's talking to, then realize he's looking at me. I'm still gripping his suit sleeve, and he's put his hand over mine. I make a show of trying to take a deep calming breath, wide eyed, and nod at him. He smiles reassuringly.

Richard moves slowly, putting the diamonds into their velvet bags, into larger bags, and then as a man walking through deep wet sand goes to the duffle on the floor. He places the diamonds within and steps back. "I think you forgot one," Dolly says. "Maybe you should double check." Mrs. Carter still holds the blue diamond in her manicured, cocktail ringed hand, where it catches the light and looks like a trapped fairy. Richard looks at Mrs. Carter, and then at Dolly pleadingly. He starts to speak, his shoulders rising, and Dolly draws her handgun with her left hand to point at him, shotgun straining against its strap, still trained on the guard. She doesn't look at me. "Go on."

Richard walks back to the table even more slowly, and picks up the velvet bag for the blue diamond. He holds it out to Mrs. Carter. "I'm sorry," he says, almost inaudibly.

"There are ways to come back from this," Mrs. Carter says in a tone that seems, for her, strangely human. "Young lady, I hope you know what you're doing."

"Well, I'd hardly tell you if I felt unsure," Dolly says with a laugh in her voice. Once the blue diamond is in the duffle, she tells Richard: "Now zip 'em up nice, thanks. No sense dropping it all on my way out." The gas mask turns and seems to consider each individual thoughtfully. "Take out your phones and drop them on top of the duffle." Nobody moves. "Now!" she barks.

There are enough people in the room to overwhelm Dolly. I hope nobody will try. The phones are dropped, one by one, including the one from my purse. Dolly considers each person again, then moves slowly to the duffle. Letting the shotgun drop on its sling, she picks the bag up on her right arm. The big door guard comes up off the floor as soon as the shotgun muzzle is no longer on the invited guests, and almost without looking, Dolly pulls the trigger on her handgun and he drops, clutching at his neck, red-faced and breathing like a freight train, compression gel rounds bouncing to the floor. The movies don't really represent just how loud a gun is. Even mentally prepared for a gunshot, they still make me shaky. Thankfully, the earbuds afford quite a lot of protection, though there's still a distant ringing in my head.

Dolly backs to the door, still brandishing the pistol. "Anybody else?" Nobody else rises to the occasion. The other women are quietly weeping, and Mrs. Carter looks as though you could milk venom from her, like a snake. "Smart crowd. You'll find your phones, eventually. I won't even look at 'em. Have a good evening now." And then she pulls the door closed behind her; the explosive gel will keep it sealed for a time.

"Oh my God," I say, letting my knees waver. Will still has my hand, and puts his other arm around my waist, guiding me to his former chair.

"I'm going to check on Clancy," he says, and the fact that the big man's name is Clancy makes me laugh, and I try to put as hysterical a note in it as possible. Mrs. Carter looks at me, practically rolls her eyes. Good. Better to be thought a flighty young thing than a suspect.

"Call the front desk," Mrs. Carter orders the barman.

"Yes ma'am." He picks up the room phone, presses a few buttons, then shakes his head. "No ringtone."

"Does anybody still have a phone?" Mrs. Carter asks. Richard, sly Richard, returns to his now empty briefcase and pulls the bottom out, revealing a small folding model. "Call the police," she says. "There's still time."

"How will the police catch them?" I ask wildly. "The police won't see where they went! It's not like they'll still be dressed like a diamond thief by the time they're out of the hotel!"

"Reading you loud and clear," Dolly says in my ear.

"Calm down," Mrs. Carter says sharply. "Stop crying," she snaps at the women, who sniffle wetly and wipe their eyes.

"He's okay," Will says, to the room. Clancy is struggling back into movement already, and tries to shrug Will off when he makes the first attempt to gain his feet. Will holds onto him with startling ease and gets him standing. "Take it easy."

The pounding begins at the door. By the time the hotel staff gets the door open, police will have arrived—detectives and patrolmen and all of it. I settle in for a long evening.

Chapter Four

It is entirely typical for the girls and I to not have contact for a few days after pulling a job; Bits and Dolly think it increases our security. I put the heist out of my mind, for the most part, and concentrate on readying my apartment for the party. Marquis shows up early on the day of, while I'm getting dressed.

"Why didn't you call me about the other night?" they demand, enveloping me in a hug at the same time.

"The police said not to talk about it, actually," I say. "Oh, and I met somebody."

"You met somebody?"

"He was there too, and was very nice before, and very comforting after. The only person who got the slightest bit hurt was the large meaty guard, Clancy, if you can imagine such a name. And I think he was mostly embarrassed."

"You do find yourself in the most interesting situations," Marquis says. "What will you wear tonight?" they ask, watching me pin my hair up.

"The patterned mauve and white dress, I think. Unless you see something you think would be preferable?"

Marquis glances over the dresses hanging in my wardrobe. "The mauve and white is charming enough."

"I hoped you'd say so." I pull the door partially closed for modesty's sake, and step into the party dress. "Zip me?"

"Did you get to see the diamonds, at least? Was the blue one magnificent?"

"They were all magnificent. It was strange, though, it seemed like most of the people there were just set dressing, not there with the slightest interest in buying. They barely looked at the stones. I'm not certain of Will, either, whether he was an innocent like me or another prop."

"Your innocence is without question, I'm sure. When are you seeing this Will again?"

"In a few days. He's taking me for coffee. Not at the whale cafe, before you ask."

"I didn't think you liked it."

"No, not really. I'm surprised you noticed."

"You're an open book to me," Marquis says, and I smile.

"Why would I expect any less?"

It's lovely having Marquis help with the final setup details, and tweak a few of the things I'd struggled with. My apartment is not large, and I deliberately don't have much furniture, but there is always a better way to arrange things, especially through a gallery owner's eyes. We drink wine spritzers and fix each other's makeup, and then the food delivery arrives, all easily managed finger food.

My guests are all people in the right sort of scene, the beautiful people who are just artsy enough to be interesting, some of whom just rich enough to be very generous with it. They arrive at the proper stages of lateness, some bringing bottles.

An alert blinks on my phone while I'm talking to my dear friend Josie, a ballet dancer who's just come off tour. "Excuse me," I say. "I'm sorry, my neighbor loses her keys all the time."

"Of course," she says, and we air kiss before she's called over to another knot of people.

I finger wave at Marquis on my way out the door, keys jingling in my other hand. How delightfully kitsch is it that my building is still physically keyed?

Down the hall, the elevator dings and Bits gets off, slouching in cargo pants and a hoodie. By the way the hoodie bulks, she's wearing a bulletproof vest under it. "What are you *doing* here?" I hiss, catching her by the arm and pulling her into the doorway of the floor's vacant apartment.

"We've got a problem," Bits says. Her hands are balled into fists, still jammed into the pockets of her hoodie. "A big enough problem that I needed to tell you face to face, not in a digital message where we could be heard."

"What are you talking about? I can't deal with this right—"

"Stop being a prima donna for a second and listen to me. The diamonds. Remember how we talked about how each diamond would have a barcode serial marker on it, for authenticity?"

"Yes." I glance back down the hallway. It's empty, my door still closed. "Why?"

"That's not what's in the barcodes of these diamonds."

I look at Bits, but her facial expression is rarely of any help. I can tell she's scared right now, but not how scared, on a scale of spiders to snipers. "What do you mean? What is it?"

"I don't know exactly, I don't have the right kind of reader. But it's some kind of encrypted data, and they may or may not be able to track it."

"What do you mean? Like RFID?"

"Maybe. It's a good guess, anyway. So I put them in an aluminum case, to cut that off. And they're...someplace safe right now. But we need to sell them quick, if it's not already be too late."

"Too late for what?"

"They might know already who we are. Where we are."

I stare at her. Open my mouth, close it. I want to tell her not to be silly. But of course they already know where I am. They sent me an invitation. Down the hall, the elevator chimes as it descends floors. "Can they do that?" I ask finally.

"I wouldn't be here if they couldn't."

"Did you tell Dolly?"

"Yeah. She's in the car."

"I can't just leave! My apartment is full of people."

"That's good, you know nobody'll expect you to leave. You have a balcony? Go get changed and then come on."

"This is just unheard of. And no, no I don't have a balcony."

"Go." For once, Bits locks eyes with me, and her gaze does not waver. The elevator chimes again, on its way back up, and I turn and hurry back to my apartment.

"Is everything okay?" Marquis asks once I slip back inside.

"Just fine, darling," I say, smiling tightly. "I do need to make some adjustments, though. My underpinnings just will not stay where they belong."

"Isn't that a trial." Marquis sails off to speak with a man at the cheese and grape plate who wears tremendous spectacles which do not seem technologically augmented in any way.

I go to my room, blessedly empty, and shut the door behind me, locking it slowly and with care so that the little click isn't heard by those nearest. I shuck off my party dress and don my riot gear, rummage in the bottom of my closet for what Dolly calls the bug-out bag. I sweep everything from my vanity into my makeup bag and jewelry box and jam them into the bug out bag. The knock on my apartment door reverberates all the way to my bedroom and I freeze, every nerve alight.

"Don't worry about it," Marquis calls out, and I clap a hand over my mouth to keep from calling out, from stopping them. I open my window and toss the bag down to Dolly, waiting on the sidewalk. Then I step back to my room door, velvet boots silent on the plush carpet.

Nobody seems to be alarmed, and there isn't much break in the conversations. I can hear both Marquis and whoever is at the door, though I can't make out what they're saying. I debate going back out to the party, trying to handle whoever is at the door. Dolly will be impatient, Bits is already in panic mode. I return to the window and look out.

When I selected my third floor apartment, I hadn't really considered a window exit. The neighbors have constructed a makeshift balcony just below me, however, a rickety eyesore made from chicken wire and pallets, and after a moment of psyching myself up, I stop thinking about it and climb out the window, hang by my hands, and drop. The balcony dips like a diving board and then holds, quivering. I climb over the edge and drop to the sidewalk, heart in my throat. Through the open window above, I hear a banging on my room door, an insistent pounding which suggests a polite knock was tried first. My wrist vibrates minutely beneath my glove; it's Marquis, I'm sure, and I hope they will understand. Dolly has me by the arm and drags me into the car. Bits is behind the wheel, gearshift already in drive, and starts moving before the door can close properly.

My wrist vibrates again, and again, and then it seems I hear a shout on the street, but I'm not sure exactly. And then Bits turns the corner down the block.

Chapter Five

"How long have you two had something like this planned?" I ask. Our safehouse is a refurbished shipping container in a sort of no man's land on the fringe of the city, between the river and several industrial parks which seem to be run entirely by robots and drones.

"I started to do it little by little once we started making money," Bits says. "We just haven't had to go to ground like this before."

"Who built it? You? Do we have to worry about other people knowing?"

"There are people who do this kind of thing, in many locations. I had it moved by drone freight after they built it."

"How do you even get wireless in here? This whole thing is beyond bizarre." I realize I've been pacing, stop. I read Marquis' messages over and over.

//Hey, open up.//
//Are you okay?//
//Wait, where are you?//
//What's going on?//
//Who are these people?//
//Call me.//
//Call me. I'm worried.//

//You need to think about what's going to happen.//

And last, but not least ominous: //They're willing to make a deal.//

"They won't do anything to Marquis," Bits says with her mouth full. There's a hot plate and enough instant ramen to choke anybody who cared less about the quality of their food than the quality of their gadgets. I think of the party food at my apartment, think about Marquis, who is probably one of my best friends in the whole world—or at least in town—and sigh.

"I certainly hope not. Marquis was on the original guest list."

"But if you think the whole showing was a coverup for the couple of people actually involved in whatever those diamonds actually are, then that won't matter and they'll realize it pretty quick," Dolly points out.

"In a perfect world," I say. *They're willing to make a deal.* "Bits, you still have no idea what the stones actually are?"

"They're actually diamonds. I just don't know what's encoded on them and haven't broken the encryption yet."

"Can't you hack it or whatever?" I wave my hand. I understand basic computer usage, my phone, household gadgets, I press buttons and they do what they're supposed to. Whatever it is Bits does when she puts that headset on is entirely beyond me, a completely different world.

"Well yeah, I'm working on it, but I need to figure out the right program, and then the right algorithms to start trying. At least the data seems static, like messing with it isn't going to erase it or do anything else terrible."

"All right, then what?"

"I guess it depends on what kind of a deal they wanna make," Dolly says. She flops onto her back on one of the fold-up futons. "They probably assume we don't have a way to find out what's encrypted on the diamonds, and they'll just offer us a chunk of change to go away. Not that I'm suggesting we work with The Man or whoever."

"More like they'll just find us and shoot us," Bits says. "Disappear us."

"I wish I knew who 'they' were, so I could refute that," I sigh. "And we just left Marquis there."

"If we'd taken the time for Marquis we wouldn't be able to have this conversation," Bits says.

"We need to—"

"We need to be goddamn careful," Dolly says. "We go out there, the crosswalk cameras will get us on the facial rec right off. Or an ATM. Or a car with a dash cam, anything."

"I'm amazed you haven't learned the benefits of these," I say, leaning over to rummage in my bag. I pull out a big square patterned scarf, large enough to cover my bare shoulders in a rain if I need it.

"I'm proud of you, learning anarchic hacker tricks." Bits grins.

"Oh, it's one of those things." Dolly doesn't like being reminded of what she already knows. I'd guess she probably has a dreadful hoodie.

"It's a matter of survival. I have several in the bag, we can each have one."

"Nah, you're the one who pulls off the starlet in a scarf look," Dolly says. "Okay, so what's the plan then? Or a first step?" We all look at each other.

"Well, I already contacted Bristol's diamond guy," Bits ventures. "Before all this went down. He might not want them now, once he sees the serial numbers aren't serial numbers." She looks down at her tablet, taps a few things. Her headset is still in its case; that's reassuring, if paranoid Bits doesn't think she needs to all-senses monitor our security situation. "We're still clear."

"If he might not want them, is it worth the risk trying to meet up?" Bits just looks at me. "Okay, or what about this: Is the fact that they're willing to make a deal an option at all?"

"It might be if we knew who 'they' were," Dolly says. "If this is Columbian drug lord shit, then no, there's no way we'll walk out of a meeting like that alive. If it's Americans recovering agent intel or something, then yeah, that's fine."

"You don't want to work with The Man but you still trust our 'Man' over any other?" I ask. Dolly shrugs, investigates the ramen options. "I think we've watched too many movies."

"What we should've done is gone to ground immediately," Bits says. "The sale was weird enough to begin with. Just a happy accident that you had a big party afterwards."

"The party has been scheduled for months," I sniff, shaking my head.

"They'll know that too."

Dolly throws her hands in the air. "Stop being so fucking ominous, Bits, they gotta have a reason to look and find out. They're not just omnipotent or omnipresent or whichever other one of those you wanna add."

"How do you know they aren't?"

"Okay. So I think we're agreeing to just try and sell the cursed things as planned?" I ask.

"Yeah, sounds like," Dolly says after a moment's pause.

"I'll message him again," Bits says. "And we should all try to get some sleep, it's late."

I'm awake in the dark for a very long time. Neither of the others make much noise, Bits fusses around on her gadgets for quite a while before all is finally silent.

Chapter Six

"I hope you know what you're doing, Miss Bristol," Baxter says. According to the peeling sign hung on his door he's a lawyer, but what Baxter really does is buy things.

"Have I ever given you reason to doubt me?" I ask as I settle myself in a seat, resisting the urge to spread a handkerchief there first. Bits places one of the little velvet bags on his desk.

"I can't say that you have, no. But this is a bigger haul than I expected from you." Baxter picks up the bag, pours some of the stones into his palm. His hands are improbably clean, nails trimmed and buffed. "How many bags of these did you say you have?"

"Four small bags like that, and then the pièce de résistance, a large blue stone."

"Lots of rocks. A big blue, you say? That one might give me trouble. We'll see." Baxter shakes his head, and spreads the diamonds in a velvet tray on top of his desk. He opens one of the drawers and pulls out a tablet with a sort of stylus plugged into it, which glows faintly green on the end when he clicks a button. "We'll find out together," he says. His eyes skim over Bits, and settle on Dolly for a moment. We're all still in riot gear, more or less, though I've unbuttoned my vest for comfort and rolled my pants legs. "Interesting cadre." I see no reason to answer. He fits a jeweler's loupe in his eye, and when he presses a button on that as well, it makes a small, high pitched noise. The lenses audibly adjust in the quiet room.

He spends some moments wanding over different parts of the diamonds and squinting, tilting his head this way and that. Then Baxter goes still.

Baxter pulls off the loupe and sweeps the diamonds back into their little bag. He shoves the bag, the tray, and both the wand and loupe at Bits.

"What is it?" I ask, getting to my feet even before Dolly does.

"Take it and get out of here. I don't even want to use equipment that's touched that."

"But what's wrong?"

"I've seen that encryption before. The stones aren't from Africa." I open my mouth to speak, but he screeches his chair back and comes around the desk, herding us out of the room like sheep, his arms spread wide. "Please, leave. Keep those in a Faraday box if you have one. If you don't have one, get one. Especially the big blue rock. I'll pretend I don't know anything when they come."

"Who's going to come?" Dolly digs her heels in, tries to pause on the foyer.

"I'm surprised they're not here already," he says, and slams the door hard enough that the sign falls onto the ground.

"Well that was...productive," I say, settling my scarf as we hurry down the cracked sidewalk to the car.

"I got some tech out of the deal, anyway," Bits says dubiously, closing her door behind her.

"Yes, we can read the information now, anyway. I've never seen him act like that, but I'm certain he'll be just fine. Baxter is used to getting rolled up with whatever investigations brush by him. I guess he got a law degree online?"

"Maybe he got it that one time he actually went to prison," Dolly says, pulling carefully into traffic. I twist in my seat to look out the back windshield past Bits, but no flashing lights or helicopters descend upon the block we've just left.

"It hardly matters now. We can wait for Bits to break the encryption and we can then decide what to do about them." Marquis hasn't texted me since last night, and it's taken all of my restraint to not text back.

"You really think the government is going to pay for them instead of just arresting us and packing us off to some mystical terrorist camp like Gitmo? Do they still have Gitmo?" Dolly asks.

"They say they don't, but whether they do or not isn't the point. There's always a Gitmo and there's always terrorists. It's integral to the nation's dialogue at this point."

"I swear, Bristles, you're involved in politics."

"She's not," Bits says quietly.

"I'm not, I promise. It's just politicians have the nicest parties, and like drinking around pretty girls while buying them drinks."

"Sure," Dolly says. Traffic thins, and Bits gets more and more edgy as we become the only car on the road. She looks around frequently, checking her tablet.

As we come to the last turn she says, "Cameras show nothing, and have shown nothing. Nobody followed us. But we'll have to leave after tonight."

"Yeah. Good," Dolly says. Once we're inside, she asks, "So what's the real problem here, other than that we stole a bunch of diamonds we can't sell? Is it Russia? Isn't Russia our ally?"

"Russia's always our allies, and then not, and then allies again. They just had a summit within the last couple of weeks. Nuclear power sanctions again. Trade sanctions, to do with human rights."

"Russia still uses old style reactors," Bits mutters.

"So what would be on the diamonds?" Dolly asks. "And were there Russians at the showing the other night? It didn't sound like it."

"I didn't think so either." Though my ear for accents could use some more work.

"Great, then it's some black ops bullshit we got ourselves in." Dolly shakes her head, but she's grinning, like this all has become more exciting than she could have hoped.

"Let's just get the data so we're aware of the decision we're making. I know a lot of people. *We* know a lot of people. We can find another buyer, I'm sure of it. Is that okay Bits? How long will that take you?"

"I have no idea," Bits says. She's already set herself up with a tray table at one of the futons and is in the process of scanning the first diamond, a plug running from the tablet to the loupe and then from the loupe to her headset. "I'll let you know when I think we need to move."

"I just want to know what kind of a world this is, where it's easier to move *diamonds* than *data*?" Dolly says. "Data's everywhere, speed of light, invisible."

"We're all living in surveillance states," Bits says. "And the diamond industry is one of the weird corners of it. Probably the certificates for these diamonds are real, and they had some-body like me layer the data into the etching. It's fucking elegant work."

"Of all the private diamond sales in all the cities in all the world," I say, but I'm the only one who's seen Casablanca.

We sit in silence for *hours*. Bits works with a concentration that cannot be broken. Dolly seems to fall asleep, and I occupy myself with magazines I've saved on my phone. It is with effort that I don't check the news, text anybody, call anybody just for the idle chatter of it. I spend so much of my time in idle chatter.

We all have a breaking point, though. "So it figures that I'm the one to bring it up, but are either of y'all bored?" Dolly asks. "I mean, other than the big ol' fearing for our mortal lives thing, this is kinda boring."

"It is," I sigh. "I can't spend endless time on the internet like Bits, and I'm not allowed to message anybody, and this is hard-ly a setup I can turn into a spa day. No offense."

"None taken," Bits says. "I've never had a spa day in my life."

"You should, they're absolutely divine!"

"Yeah I never have either," Dolly says.

"Bits, can't we do *something*? I know you don't want us to come and go to much—I understand that, I really do—but at least you've had the diamonds to occupy you..."

Bits pushes her headset up onto the top of her head, looks between Dolly and I. She hesitates, and I think she's going to make one of her very adult and reasonable arguments how, for safety and security's sake, we have to stay here and be as quiet as church mice, and we can just do something tomorrow once we change locations. I try to anticipate her argument, formu-late a response regarding just how innocuous it would be for us to go to a convenience store, or even a food truck, something, anything in the world. The three of us are simply too small in this big city to be so easily tracked. In fact, with the diamonds all boxed up, they may never track us again.

But Bits knows we're up against the boundaries of Dolly containment. "So what do you want to do?" she asks finally. "Neither of you plays video games, or I'd say we can go to this underground arcade. It's dark out now, and they're safe people. I trust them. One last trip isn't going to be the dealbreaker."

"An arcade would be fun," I say. I can people watch in an arcade, at the very least, and Dolly can shoot things. "Do you mean standup machines that we put actual coins in."

"They're modified for tokens," Bits says. "But yeah."

"Fuck it, I'm in," Dolly says.

Chapter Seven

It's a relief to just be able to go out with the specific intent to have some fun and relax. Though we engage in criminal activities for fun and profit, I'm not exactly well suited to the stresses of being on the lam, looking over my shoulder at every move. I chose this, yes, but there are degrees. Bits drives by the light of the conveniently full moon and the light pollution from the looming city, and we don't see another car until she parks in a convenience store lot. Moths and other bugs of the night swarm about the LEDs, and when we get out of the car, our skin seems strange and blue beneath the abrasive light.

Bits leads us away from the convenience store, behind it and down a shadow-layered alleyway with fire escapes looming overhead. "So, this arcade isn't entirely legal," she says as we reach a yellow-lit steel security door. She knocks on the door and red shreds of paint come away on the knuckles of her gloves. Even though this is supposed to be a fun time, none of us relax far enough to take off our gear, not even me.

"I don't think any of us will even pretend we're surprised," I say.

"Not even a little bit," Dolly agrees. At least she's only carrying one gun, settled in the slide holster up her sleeve.

"That just means it's safer for us," Bits says. "Not a single person here is going to want to talk to any cops."

"What about feds or Russian spies?"

"I guess that depends on the deals they offer."

The door swings open, and what I can only assume is a bouncer surveys us. He's Clancy sized or larger, wearing a bulletproof vest and a sawed-off shotgun in a thigh holster.

"You girls lost?" He asks. His voice is falsely gruff, and I notice the laugh lines extending from behind his sunglasses.

"Come off it, Charlie, we're here to play." Bits shoves her anti-surveillance hood back.

A smile breaks on his face. "Bitsy, didn't see you there! Blondie here and the girl with the gun took up my attention. Where've you been?"

"It's a long story, Charlie. Maybe another time."

Charlie shrugs. "Well, come on in!" We file in, and he looks down the dark alley before pulling the door shut. As I pass him, I can see the glow of a heads up display on the insides of the sunglass lenses. The light in the hallway is intermittent, and the walls are all exposed studs, conduit. The whole building seems to hum.

"What's new?" Bits asks.

"Got in some pinball machines from a Japanese scrapyard, and a refurbished xBox with fighting games on it," he says.

"Which version?"

"Of xBox? That's not my department, you know that. Ask Lockhart."

"Will do." Bits leads the way down the hallway, the hum growing stronger. The fire door opens onto a metal scaffolded stairway, and the space below us glows like a nest of fireflies.

Maybe this building used to be a factory or something, the floor seems huge and entirely open. Fifty or more brightly colored arcade machines are arranged in lines, along with pinball machines, skee ball, even one antique pair of dance pads. Christmas lights rope around many of the upright surfaces, and they have a little bar, with a popcorn machine, a fryer, and a hotplate.

As we descend the stairs, a knot of people close in near one of the arcade machines, their voices raised. Dolly starts to straighten her gun arm, and behind her, I put a hand on her shoulder. Another bouncer, this one far more sour looking, wades into the crowd and pulls apart two scrapping teens in ripped jeans, big stomping boots, and shirts with cartoon characters on them.

"No fighting!" the bouncer roars as he holds them apart like two cats that had gotten into a tangle. He thankfully relied on his hands for this; he has a shotgun too. "It's only a game. It's only ever a game. If you can't play nice, you can't come here no more." He gives them a shake, his tattooed muscles flexing. "Can you kids play nice?"

One of them nods, and the other one, the one with a bloody nose, manages a sullen, "Yes."

"That's good then." He drops them to their feet, and while they still stagger, off balance, claps them each on the back in a show of goodwill. The gathered teens around them keep them from falling, and then the crowd disperses again. The kid with the bloody nose wipes it on the back of his hand, then wipes his hand on his jeans, while the other boy walks off in a different direction.

"Is there anything in particular you want to play?" Bits asks, bright eyed but almost shy.

"When I was a kid," Dolly says meditatively, "they came out with a re-re-mastered console, an emulator of one of the first ones that they came out with in the 20th. There was a game on it that seemed so simple; you shot ducks like you were out on a lake, but if you missed, a dog—I guess it was supposed to be a retriever—would pop up and laugh at you. I guess TV's didn't work the way they used to, so it went away, and then they came out with the next generation of interactive TV's and somebody did the game again."

"Of course your favored video game is a shooting one," I say.

"Aw, come on," Dolly says, and actually looks hurt. "It's like, the first hunting game. Not a people shooting game."

"I don't think they have that one," Bits says. "Or they didn't."

"You two go on," I say. "I'll find a way to occupy myself."

"If you say so," Bits says dubiously, Dolly already urging her away.

I turn my attention to the people. The teens still trying to figure out who they are and what they want, the young professionals who, really, are in much the same boat as the teens except they're expected to be adults on a directed path by now. A few people who are older, silver starting to thread through their hair. I wander to the bar, drawn by the carnival scent of freshly popped popcorn, and ask for that and a water.

"No water today," says the slouching girl behind the bar. "You want a beer?"

"I guess," I say. I don't, but there is unlikely to be anything else I'd prefer to drink.

"You have cash?" The girl asks, still not moving towards the plastic cooler set on the floor behind her, leaking a thin stream of water across the concrete, or the popcorn machine.

"I do," I say. "Or I think I do." It is rare for me to have cash, actually, and I rummage in my cargo pockets, finally coming up with a wadded handful of bills, their denomination holographs flashing weak blue numbers around my fingers. "How much?"

"Ten." I count it out. "Not into the games?" she asks. I simply don't have the look.

"It's not something I ever got into. I love the atmosphere, though," I offer. The entire feeling here is of a surreptitious party, a joy that can't be scratched out.

"Yeah, Lockhart built it, more or less, but Charlie and Goose are necessary muscle. We make enough scratch to keep things going, somehow. I don't really know how Lockhart does it, to be honest, but sometimes I think the less I know the better."

"You're talking about everybody else, what's your name?" I ask, popping the tab on my dripping beer, licking the moisture off my thumb.

"Jane. I just work for the free tokens. Keeps me off the streets, right?" She shrugs and gave a short little laugh.

"You should give yourself more credit. A place like this can be intimidating, and yet you both work and play here. I think it's pretty wonderful."

"Well thanks for the pep talk." Jane walks off to help another customer, but her smile is a little bit different.

I find a chair and table. The popcorn is very good and the beer is a nice surprise, actually; some kind of artisanal craft brew I've never heard of. I pull out my non wrist phone to scan the QR code, and at that moment it buzzes in my hand. Reflexively, I answer it, voice only. "Bon soir."

"Is this the lovely lady I met in unfortunate circumstances the other night?" I can't place the voice for a split second, and then it clicks.

"If this is Will, then yes, it is! I'm so glad you called." A small cheer goes up from the nearby, larger crowd; apparently Dolly and Bits have reached some kind of achievement never before seen, and are still going.

"Is this a bad time? It seems loud where you are."

"I can still hear you, but give me a moment to get someplace a bit more serene. You know how those impromptu city parties can get; I don't even know who most of these people are."

"Well, I find it hard to believe there's anywhere you would feel out of place."

"Flatterer." I wander back towards the bar. Jane looks at me questioningly, looks at the phone, and then points at a door I hadn't noticed. I mouth 'thank you' and push through it into another dark hallway, keeping my toe in the opening so it won't lock behind me.

"Is it flattery if it's the truth?"

"Now we're getting metaphysical." I'm able to flirt emptily and with ease for a very long time, in all manner of circumstances, but Will's timing is disquieting. "But there must be a reason you called?"

"I wanted to know when I could see you again."

"Oh, I did hope you would say that," I say. "I do regret, I'm going to have to reschedule our coffee. Did you have something in mind next week maybe?"

"Just dinner in a nice restaurant."

"I think that would be very nice."

"I hope so." Will pauses, and that niggling unease just keeps rising. I shift my weight and peer out through the door back into the arcade. I can see Dolly from this angle, barely. I can also see up the stairs to the door where we entered. It seems to me the window in that door should be pretty dark. Or was there a light right at the entryway? I can't remember, and I should remember, but there's light there now, pale white.

"Will, I think I have to let you go," I say carefully.

"I'm sorry to hear that," Will says. "Are you alright? Do you need anything?" It seems a strange way to phrase things, a strange thing to ask.

"I'm not really sure," I say. "Have you heard anything more about...the other night?"

"Some, yes, though not from the police who talked to us. I may have spoken to Richard for a time, about the provenance of those diamonds."

"To Richard?" I ask sharply.

"To Richard. He'd have the best information, wouldn't you say?"

"Him or Mrs. Carter."

"Clever girl," he says and the sound in the background of his call changes just slightly, and I hear a fountain. Indoor fountains are unusual, but I can think of several in the city. Including at Marquis' gallery.

"This might sound strange, Will darling, but where are you right now?"

"Oh, at this little place downtown. Full of the most interesting artwork at the moment. Some eclectic people as well. Do you know it?"

"I think I might." I'm trying to keep my voice breezy. "Is it the place down on Market that replaced the front windows with large stained glass pieces?"

"That's the one! The gallery owner is most interesting. Marquis? And I think Marquis knows you quite well."

"Why yes, we're very good friends. I was at the gathering the other night in Marquis' stead, as I'm sure you know by now."

"Yes, we're well aware." Will pauses significantly, and I wonder if he practiced for this. "We're going to need those diamonds," he says. "It's in your best interests, and your accomplices. You're in a great deal of danger right now, you see."

"Am I? I'm rather alarmed that you've asked me for dinner and then begun to threaten me." The light outside that upstairs door is getting brighter. I tuck the phone between my ear and shoulder and use my wrist phone to send Bits a message.

//We need to pull the plug. Alternate exit by the bar.//

"Chelsea, I'm not threatening you. I represent safety. But there is a threat against you, from other interested parties."

"I see. You understand this is rather sudden." I see Dolly's posture change.

"I do. But your position is very near to being compromised, if it hasn't been already."

"And you say your people aren't after us, but rather a third party?"

"Yes. The party which is most interested in recovering those diamonds in the first place."

"And you're saying you can offer us help or asylum or something along those lines."

"In the immediate sense, yes. In the future legal sense, perhaps not. But, in order to have a future..."

"Oh, we were doing so well, and that was so very indelicate." Bits and Dolly are here with me in the dark hallway, and we let the door swing shut. It does lock. "Now, I'm sorry darling, I do have to let you go this time. Is this the number where you can best be reached?"

"It is, but I don't think you understand..." I hang up on him. The phone buzzes immediately, an angry hornet in my palm, and I shut it down entirely and drop it into one of my vest pockets.

"Who was that?"

"Will from the hotel room. He's with the ones who claim to be the good guys, and whoever the bad guys are, they're at the top of the stairs outside, waiting for some go sign."

"Oh shit, Charlie," Bits murmurs, her eyes going big and voice catching.

"With luck they tased him and left him outside," Dolly says. "Quieter and takes less time. Now let's get out of here. How do you think they found us?"

"I don't know, but we need to get to the car and then figure that out quick, because if they did it once they can do it again. I especially don't know why they didn't before now."

"Turn off all your devices," Bits says. She doesn't give me a look, but she may as well have. "Hopefully they didn't find the car."

We creep through the dark hallway, passing through spears of light from nail holes in the walls, and when the uproar of the raid kicks into a high volume, we run.

We reach an outside door, and Bits creeps out first, nearly silent. She comes back and motions for us to follow, and we go down another alley, until we once again come to the convenience store. I look back as we drive away, but the dark alleyways don't look any different from before, even as the first gunshots crack open the night.

Chapter Eight

The shipping container hideout and surrounding area seem normal, but Bits begins to pack. "Bits, it's three in the morning. A girl needs her beauty sleep." I try very hard to keep the whine out of my voice.

"We don't know how they caught up to us. And now we know what they'll do if they find us," Bits says, shoving a duffle bag into my hands. "We need to move now, because we have no idea whether this location is compromised as well. We power up zero devices until we get to the next place. Dolly, are you listening?"

Dolly, already packed, stands at the doorway looking through the peephole, her e cigarette dangling from the corner of her mouth. "Sounds good," she says laconically. "Nobody's on the road, if that'll settle your biscuits at all."

"It will not." Bits doesn't even crack a smile, seems on the verge of tears. I wonder how well she knows the arcade people. "I'll get us new burner phones. Keep your old ones, but I think that's how they tracked us, and that's why it took so long."

"Explain," Dolly says. Her e cigarette smells like cedar and something else I can't quite place.

"We all had our phones on us, any number of wireless devices. The closest tower that serviced the hotel would have records of everything that connected. It takes time to narrow down who would've been in specific rooms, but..."

Dolly nods. "As easy as that."

"Maybe I'm just making it sound too easy," Bits says.

"Perhaps it's that you make it sound very easy for the people with the right equipment and capabilities," I say thoughtfully. Bits does not make wild guesses; she can track me by anything I wear on a regular basis, from my earbuds to my bracelet phone. "Where is the next location?" I ask. "Perhaps a hotel? With things like a toilet and running water?"

"It is, actually." Bits finally stops her whirlwind, surveys the shipping container. "I think that's everything. Load up." Bits drives again; she's the one with the safe house algorithm. She's already hacked the license plate, so the holo displays another vehicle's. The tint of the windows is just enough to keep us from being instantly recognizable, but isn't so dark as to draw immediate suspicion.

"You've done this a number of times before you met us, I take it?" I ask.

"Yeah, kind of. My folks were survivalists, so pretty low tech. But once I started getting my hands on junked computers and rebuilding them, I couldn't stay out there in the woods anymore. I brought the paranoia with me, though."

I stare at her, mystified. "Paranoia about what, out in the woods? There aren't many people living outside cities anymore, are there?"

Dolly snorts. "There's plenty of people still living outside cities," she says. "Maybe not in the woods like Bitsy's folks, but there's all that real estate off the grid, and not everybody is a big fan of the way city things run. And there are things other than people to be worried about."

"You're a country mouse too, Dolly? Why haven't we ever talked about this?"

She shrugs. "It just never came up."

"Well." I am, for once, flummoxed. "I didn't mean for the two of you to think you couldn't talk about yourselves."

"It doesn't matter," Bits says. "What matters is getting out of this mess. Or managing this mess. Whatever you want to say about it."

We're silent for several blocks. I think of the things I would like to do instead of being driven to ground in the city. Moving freely about in the manner I am accustomed is high on the list. A nice long bath, with scented oils.

The hotel is a step up from a coffin hotel, which was my quiet fear. Check in is automated, and helpful robots handed us heated towels and snacks before we leave the lobby to go to our suite. "This was one of the very first robot hotels in the country," Bits says. "Japan had them for a couple of years before we did, and as always, we were happy to let them refine the process first before adopting it. There's another one by the airport, nicer for all of the business travelers, but then of course it's higher traffic."

"It's perfectly fine. I just hope there's a tub."

"Some have them and some don't."

The hotel is not multi floored in the traditional sense, but a number of split levels with long hallways, no stairs. The carpet is thin and lacks much texture, and is probably highly cleanable by whatever robot is designed for that as well. I can't imagine what a property this size must have cost, when it was built, though perhaps it had been in one of the early century recessions which drove the real estate market to its knees. There seem to be gardens outside, with little solar lamps. I imagine what it must look in daylight, perhaps overtures at Japanese aesthetics, with things like a koi pond and a little red bridge over it, stands of bamboo, thoughtfully placed shrines and vending machines for incense and other offerings.

Our suite seems very far from the hotel lobby, and I can see why once we're inside. I peel back the shade over the back window, and there's a whole separate parking lot out there, a property fence, and then a road beyond. Bits selected this suite for its means of escape. I am beginning to think perhaps I have not devoted enough thought in life to means of escape.

The beds are futons, though so different from the shipping container futons it's difficult to imagine why they would be called the same word. The mattresses are far thicker, the frames crafted with an attention to detail instead of just pipes welded together. Bits does a short tour of the room as we set down our bags, a device in her hand that I can't remember having seen before. It is *very* hard, trying to keep track of Bits's gadgets. "What's that for?" I ask finally, as Bits folds the thing up and puts it away, apparently satisfied.

"It checks for bugs. Listening devices, wifi detectors, credit skimmers, all of that. Nothing is here though. We can relax and go to sleep now."

"Aye aye captain," I say with a smile. I crawl across the first futon I come to, then sit up and take my boots off, dropping them to the floor. I'm tired, but not too tired to be decent. I unhook my bra under my shirt, wiggle my arms through the straps and pull it clear, dropping it on the floor as well.

"Tomorrow will be better," Dolly says. "We'll know more. Maybe Bits can find out who Will is, and who came to the arcade last night."

"I'm sure everything will be fine," I say around a yawn, covering my mouth. "I'm sure I can't hold another thought in my head right now, though. I hope everybody sleeps well."

It isn't a surprise that I sleep late the next day, or that Dolly does too. It is a surprise that Bits is up very early, slipping out to get new phones and who knows what other technology, but also coffee and freshly made breakfast sandwiches from a cafe whose name I don't recognize

"I figured you'd rebel sooner or later if we were just eating vending machine and prefab stuff," Bits says. "Though the vending machine just down the hall has that really good canned coffee, that you can have hot or cold, in like thirteen flavors."

"Canned hot coffee?" I'm curious but dubious, though I happily accept one of the takeout cups.

"Don't knock it 'til you've tried it," Dolly says, her sandwich already half gone. "And hey, we do have a tub."

"Oh good. I'll have a nice soak after we eat. Is there anything we can do to help you, Bits?"

"No, but thanks for asking anyway," Bits says.

"Maybe I'll take a walk around the grounds, investigate our vending machine situation." Dolly pulls out her ponytail and scrapes her hair back again. "How many other bodies do we seem to have in house?" she asks.

"Not very many. A couple of professionals, and maybe a couple of people having an affair, so all in all nobody that's going to bother us." Bits is already setting up the equipment.

I'm so tired of riot gear; I'll wear a dress and heels today, and it will be fine. I'll make it be fine. I can run in heels almost as well as I can in boots anyway; it comes both from practice and well-made shoes. Everything is practice. When not on the run, I practice conversation in front of my augmented smart mirror, tracking when I tip my chin, or widen my eyes, the degrees of smile. Gestures. Signature words. Before I knew more French, I used to intersperse French words into speech, but it never quite struck the right note.

I step into the bathroom and slide the door shut behind me. The tub is a step in whirlpool, more than I could have hoped for. I don't have much with me that can be considered bath oils, but there are a number of small bottles on the counter, and bath bombs, labeled roses and sandalwood, wrapped in a crackly imitation of cellophane, with golden ribbons, the whole thing designed to dissolve.

I have some indistinct plan of retiring to a warm and trendy place while I'm still young, though old enough to be taken seriously. I've never been to Morocco, but I've developed a fascination for it, hunting down articles, watching travel specials, trying the food when I can. I'm not certain what the exact allure is, but it's a name to hang a dream on, a place to yearn for the sights and smells of, the sound of people talking, the sight of sunlight on foreign walls.

My problem is I spend a lot of money, even as I'm trying to save money. I can access my savings account, but at great inconvenience, so the balance grows steadily despite myself. Riot gear is expensive, and parties, and good makeup, even without buying quite so many guns and gizmos like Bits and Dolly.

Relaxing into the perfumed water, I hear the hotel room door close. Dolly going for her walk, I suppose. Though really, if we were to be caught right now, maybe I would be relieved. I don't want to be on the run, I want to still be living in that gray area between legal and illegal, where I can have fun and live my casual life.

The bathroom door isn't kicked in, and Bits doesn't raise any kind of alarm, and I finish out my bath in dozy peace. The attached blowdryer in the bathroom is a compact ceramic one and surprisingly good, and I apply my makeup with the usual care. Bits has done something with our devices, to forward texts and calls without alerting any potential watchers that the old phones had been used at all, and I open my new phone to check my messages. I do miss my wrist unit; even with a stack of delicate bangle charm bracelets, my arm feels light, and I slide a ring onto my middle finger as well, to compensate, a heavy silver band made of an antique ornate spoon, scrolled seashells and just the right amount of classy tarnish.

I have a wide range of casual acquaintances, which makes for many casual invitations to come to a gallery, or a club, or an afternoon coffee. Marquis sent me a number of messages; hopefully they're all right and not just bait. A couple of exes had sent their usual things, gestures that they would be in town and would love to take me out for dinner.

And Will.

Will reiterated that he would love to take me out for drinks, dinner. It isn't just because we are somewhat entangled due to business—but the business end of things is very important, and he needs to speak to me further on that matter. Recover the package. He claims that neither I nor and my associates would be in any trouble, and I sigh. When has anything ever been that easy?

Chapter Nine

When I leave the steaming bathroom, Bits is in much the same position, cross legged on a futon and hunched over in a VR headset, surrounded by all the other accompanying tech. Dolly is still gone, the cedar smell of e cigarette remaining in her wake, and I load the little combo washer/dryer in the corner.

//Learn anything new?// I text Bits, thinking that it's better than speaking to her at this moment, but she answers me out loud without otherwise moving.

"Did you know that something like four of the Russian imperial family's Faberge eggs are lost?"

"I'd heard that, in fact. What's that have to do with our diamonds?"

"One of the diamonds has data that claims to reflect the location of those four eggs," Bits says. "Another discusses weapons caches after a number of disarmament treaties were signed." There is a long pause, and I have the time to set out my manicure equipment, the files, the cuticle cream, the polishes to redo French nails, when Bits speaks again. The blue diamond is on the table in front of her. "Did you know Russia had a system called Dead Hand, or Perimeter, which meant

Moscow could respond to nuclear attack even if all of the command structure was gone?"

"I did not."

"It's still operational."

I pause, three nails into my left hand. "Still operational," I repeat. My grasp of the dates is fuzzy, but it seems such a thing would've been constructed early to mid 20th. For it to still be operational more than a hundred years later is chilling.

"This one has maps of the bunkers under Moscow. And there's another datacode, even further inside the facets, not just surface readable like the other ones. I think...well I don't know. I guess they wouldn't be launch codes. Maybe they're disarm codes?"

"For the Perimeter?"

"I think. I don't want to make faulty assumptions."

"What do other less impressive diamonds say?"

"Locations where subs were dumped in the arctic circle, though I guess they probably floated away by now, when the ice melted." Bits pauses, and I force myself to wait again, finishing my left hand and moving to my right, which is always a little bit more tricky. "Brand new planes that were built and then never flown, including a suborbital hypersonic jet meant to launch nuclear missiles."

"What is it with governments and their nuclear weapons? I thought the scorched earth approach had fallen out of vogue decades ago."

"It's all about perceived threat. Um. Mutually assured destruction used to be what people said kept everything safe. You bomb me, I'll bomb you, and then nobody can have anything."

"Just lovely. Simply marvelous politics."

"Well, they didn't have you yet," Bits says with a small smirk

My new phone buzzes, and I call up the message, careful of my nails. It's from Dolly.

//They have a fortune telling machine, come check it out.//

The phone buzzes again as a picture arrives of a neon AR spread of tarot cards.

If nothing else, it'll be a fascinating diversion. In the slummy apartment building where I grew up there was a woman who read tarot for people. The scarier the reading, the less she'd charge you for it, and people ironclad trusted her, but I'm still not sure any of her readings were accurate, or just what was bound to happen in the first place. She always knew I would leave.

//Where is that?// I reply.

//Right here in the hotel. Um. Take a left out of our door, take the first right, go through the water garden, and then right again.//

//Let me finish my nails, I'm almost done with my right hand.//

"Dolly found a fortune telling machine," I say to Bits.

"That doesn't surprise me," she says, her tone distant again. I assumed she saved the blue diamond for last, but she's moving the scanner over some of the smaller ones. "Go see it, and then bring Dolly back. We need to talk about whether we should call your Will and take their deal."

"He's hardly mine," I say, rolling up the manicure kit.

"He seems to have taken quite the liking to you."

"How would you—" I pause, staring at Bits's face, which is expressionless under the VR headset. Then I sigh and put my things away. "See you soon," I say, but Bits doesn't react.

A robot vacuum vrooms its way down the hallway, bouncing between the walls, beeping cheerfully when I step over it. There are a surprising number of windows as I walk through the hotel, shedding lots of golden morning light into the hallways. The water garden is quite lovely, little rainbows forming around the sprays, and a number of hummingbird feeders are interspersed through the space. The tiny, jewel-like birds flit about almost too fast to track. Or they're holograms or drones for the same eye pleasing effect; I'm entirely uncertain.

There are many, many vending machines through the hotel. Coffee ones, as Bits described. Clothing ones, for easily capsule-able clothing like bras, tops, underwear. I linger at the clothing ones for a time, then dig out a prepaid credit card. I've had a vending machine dress before and found it quite comfortable, in fact. This machine has a line of peacock patterned ones for a reasonable price, and I dial in my size and retrieve the plastic capsule.

There is plenty of food I don't want and won't eat, basic toiletries, and phones. I also get a little vial of hyacinth perfume from a French machine. I only had a little spray bottle of Chanel in my makeup kit and though the Chanel is my everyday perfume, I prefer to wear hyacinths when it rains, and I have a very strong feeling it will rain soon.

I turn the corner and Dolly stands there, e cigarette still glowing, in front of the fortune teller, labeled Madame Sosostris. I have a moment to wonder over the poetry of it.

"Have you tried it yet?" I ask.

"Me? Nah. Even if it is a game the idea kinda freaks me out."

"Oh, there's actually something in this world that freaks you out? How good to know."

"Like you thought I was some kind of machine."

"No, but you don't let us in very much, do you."

"I'm willing to say none of us lets people in very much. You seem to, but mostly it's just icing."

"Icing," I repeat, with a little bemused smile. It's the one I practiced when trying not to seem hurt, surprised, or angry. Dolly's right, though, in an unusually incisive way. I protect myself with layers of icing, pleasantness, decoration, that I expect others to freely consume. I keep the cake hidden for myself. "Well anyway, I don't typically have tarot readings, so this will be quite the experience."

"What's your fortune telling of choice then, princess?" Dolly asks, leaning against the wall across the hall from the machine. "Assuming you have one."

"Tea leaves or coffee grounds. The way Turkish coffee is made, and served, makes it my preferred tradition. You drink your cup of coffee with the fortuneteller and then they read your grounds. You can have it sweetened if you'd like—the coffee not the fortune—but milk does not typically enter the equation."

"Never heard of it," Dolly says. "Though I guess that shouldn't surprise me. Tea, yeah."

I shrug. "There are people who have a pack of cards passed down through generations. There are people who cast stones."

"I somehow didn't expect you to be into woo woo stuff like this."

"Some women like yoga, or pilates, or meditation. I like getting my fortune told."

"Do you ever do it yourself?"

"I pretended with a pack of playing cards when I was little, but no, I don't feel the spark."

"Interesting." Dolly takes another drag on her e cigarette.

I examine the controls. Madame Sosostris can do a number of different readings, from a basic three card past-present-future all the way up to the far more involved Celtic Cross. For the fun of it, I just pick three cards. I hardly want something involved with Dolly watching and smirking. It's also possible to select a preferred deck, but I just leave the default Rider-Waite set. Then I run my card, and the machine comes into further neon life, with an elaborate light show of shuffling cards before three are holographically drawn onto the front of the machine, their pink plaid backs an unexpected contrast. I've never given much thought to what the backs of tarot cards might look like.

The first card, labeled "The Recent Past," is the Chariot, which has to do with overcoming obstacles, and I give kind of a little laugh.

"What?" Dolly asks.

"Can you see it from there?"

"Not really. Won't mean anything anyway."

"Suit yourself. I thought you'd be more invested, considering you called me out here." The second card is The High Priestess, representing "The Present." The High Priestess emphasizes trusting one's intuition and keeping communication lines open, both sentiments I firmly endorse. And then the final card, "The Future", the Four of Pentacles, predicting the likely outcome: in order to secure wealth, we may be greedy or malicious.

Once all three cards are face up, the figures on them also stand up from the card surfaces, and the small holographs play out a little story based on the figures present and the meanings of the card positions. Dolly laughs, and the machine offered the option to save the reading to my device, and I select that, waving my phone for the data.

"Well that was something," Dolly says. "We'll see how things turn out, anyway. Greedy and malicious, it says."

"We *have* stolen a tremendous number of diamonds," I say thoughtfully. "Should we bring Bits some dreadful snacks, to raise her spirits? I don't remember the last time I saw her eat."

"That's a good idea. And I guess she has all the data read now?"

"I'm not entirely sure, but I don't doubt she'll be happy to regale us with all of that information."

"We just need some bullet points and an endgame, I think. Less of this hiding out shit, more collecting our money. I wanna get on with my life."

I laugh. "I'm not sure I've ever agreed with you more."

Chapter Ten

"**B**reak it down, Bits," Dolly says. "Who're the players? Who're the good guys?"

"Dolly, there are *never* clear-cut good guys," Bits says. The headset has left lines on her face, and her eyes are droopy, out of focus.

"You've done an unbelievable amount of work for us, Bits," I say. "Don't you want to lie down first, have a nap, and then we can form a game plan?"

Bits takes one of the snack bags and shakes some chips into her hand. "Maybe. I'll tell you some stuff first. I did some digging online, deep web stuff, and I think whoever smuggled the diamonds might have been working both sides all along—a Russian operative feeding intel to other countries. Our original smuggler might have been in an artsy or performance crowd, and had access to high level bad guys, for lack of a better term, who might have been loose with their secrets and their phones and passwords and stuff."

"That's a substantial bit of information," I say.

Bits nods for a little too long, chewing more chips. I'm coming to the unfortunate conclusion that they are cricket chips, not corn chips. "So what we have are a lot of secrets that would have once been called Soviet, in the Cold War. Which is supposed to have ended, but I'm not sure it ever did, based on everything ever. I mean, it never got hot. But it never actually went away either. Maybe it's a shadow war?"

"That's a good thing to call it," I consider taking one of Dolly's e cigarettes, for something to do, or to soothe my nerves. That's what they're for, isn't it?

"And so the U.S. might have been the intended buyer for them. But after the original smuggler lost possession of them, it was to somebody who was more interested in selling them to the highest bidder."

"So here's a thing, did we hear about this job because diamonds are flashy and expensive, or because somebody was actually peddling the information?" Dolly asks. Bits shrugs with open arms, offers the chips around. I shake my head, Dolly takes a handful.

"I looked into Will a little bit. He's American. Born in Virginia, went to work in Washington after college."

"He was very nice when we were robbed by a ruffian," I say with a smile. "Comforting."

"He's easy on the eyes, I'll tell you that," Dolly says.

"He was very eager to meet when we spoke last night. I could definitely get him someplace public and see what we can get out of him. Discuss this deal of his."

"I wasn't going to ask you to, but..." Bits trails off.

"You do computers, Dolly does guns, and I manage people. I'll call him once we're done with our discussion."

"Bitsy, where'd you find this job again?"

"The tip was on a deep web message board, same as I've found a lot of our other stuff." Bits shrugs. "No way to know who posted it. Though even if I didn't hear about it online,

Bristol would've heard about it through Marquis. They sent re-al life invitations. This whole thing is weird."

Dolly frowns. "Hey Bristles, you don't think Marquis...?"

"I think Marquis fit the appearance they wanted to culti-vate for the sale."

"Okay, now I'm gonna crash for like, twelve hours. See if Will wants to take you out after that, so we can listen in and keep our eyes open," Bits says.

"I will. Sleep well."

She doesn't even kick her boots off, just puts the bag of chips down, curls up, and falls asleep. I wonder if some of the computer equipment might even still be attached to her. Dol-ly turns on the television, pokes at the remote until the sound routes through her earbuds instead of in the room. "I'll be here if anybody needs me."

"I think I'll make my call from that water garden. With all the hummingbirds."

"Turn all your shit off afterwards," Bits mumbles. "Just the call will give them a lot of intel, but maybe not enough to come knocking."

"Of course."

WILL ANSWERS ON THE first ring. "It's so good to hear from you," he says warmly.

"Good afternoon, Will." I've settled on a bench by one of the waterfalls, with a view of three hummingbird feeders. Maybe I'll be able to tell if they're real or not by the end of things.

"I trust everything went well last night?"

"We made our hasty retreat, if that's what you mean. I do appreciate the warning, though."

"You're very welcome." I wait. So much of a conversation depends on the pauses, on what isn't said. "So, I imagine you're getting tired of campfire food and would like a more civilized experience?"

"Campfire food?" I laugh. "Yes, it is dreadful. Civilization seems very nice about now. I'm not used to roughing it in any sense of the word."

"No, a woman like you enjoys reasonable comforts," he says. "And you deserve them. Luxuries, even."

"And now you're flattering me again."

"Do you have a restaurant in mind? You can choose wherever you'd like."

Wherever I'd like opens up infinite possibilities. I consider, and then name a newer place with a very experimental chef I heard about before all of this diamond business got started. "I'm not sure what the menu will be, of course. Though that's part of the adventure of it."

"Of course. I went to his mentor's restaurant in Chicago and it was an...experience. I guess the food was good. I had to get a burger after. The problem with all that gourmet stuff is they don't, in the end, give you very much food at all. They give you the idea of food. The notion that one day your stomach might be full."

"Will, are you a poet?"

"Some things make me wax poetic. Like burgers."

"Burgers," I say, rolling my eyes. He laughs.

"What can I say, I like things simple. And you do know what we intend to discuss over dinner?"

"Our possible future together? Perhaps certain luxuries?"

"Something like that." He laughs again. "I think we understand each other."

"Perhaps." He does seem very comfortable. Maybe he's overconfident, or maybe he has a file on me.

"So I'll pick you up around six?" Overconfident, then.

"I'll meet you there at eight o'clock. That's when the second seating begins."

"As you say. Until tonight, then."

"Until tonight." I hang up, turn off all of my devices. I'll redo my makeup, more elaborately. False eyelashes, a bolder red lipstick. I look up at the sky; I really should have checked the weather before calling Will, and I can't turn the phone back on now, but it does seem as though it might rain. I'll wear my hyacinth perfume, and my new dress. My turtlescale camisole will suffice, my usual stockings and hair pins.

I'm still planning, not daydreaming precisely, when Dolly comes to find me under the darkening sky. "Did you know Bits snores?" she asks.

"I'm sure we all do under enough duress." I am, in fact, confident that I do not snore.

"Depends on how I'm laying," Dolly says. She turn towards movement, and watches a trio of hummingbirds flit onto the nearest feeder and flit away again. "Are those real?"

"I've been trying to figure that out. I can't quite tell."

"They got robot bees and stuff now. Pollinators. Because so many of them died. They look like regular bees, I guess because they need to be the right shape to fit into flowers and rub up against the right stuff. Just making them discs or whatever didn't work."

"That's both sad and charming. I don't know anything about what happened with the bees."

"Back home we had a tiny little hive. But there was a big factory farm nearby with the bee drones. Robot bees."

"I thought that was what you meant."

"They tried to color 'em differently too, so it's kind of obvious when you see them, unlike the hummingbirds. Little articulate jewel toned robot bees. Though I guess there's naturally blue bees some places? Or there were. These ones didn't have stingers, though, that was a big difference. They still knew if you caught one."

"What happened if you caught one?"

"If it was just to see it, no big deal. The pollen gets stored in little leg capsules I guess, so just touching them doesn't ruin everything. But if you keep it from going home, or you break it on purpose or catch a bunch of 'em, they make trouble for you."

"The factory farm?"

"And the local government, since that's where a lotta the kickbacks came from. It's under some kind of FDA umbrella. What we learned in school isn't always what's true."

I try to think what "make trouble" means. Get ticketed? Then I realize Dolly said "had" a small hive. Not "has."

"Oh," I say.

"Yeah," Dolly says, dragging on her e cigarette. "That's not when I left home, but it wasn't long after. Couldn't get work there, and even though the bees made us so little, that income buffer was important. So now I'm here, and we do what we do."

"It seems amazing to me that we never asked each other anything before. Talked about why we were in this."

"What were we gonna do, have a slumber party and do each other's hair and nails while talking about boys and ruined families or whatever? No thanks."

"That isn't exactly what I meant."

"No, and that probably wasn't fair, so I'm sorry. But still. Who wants to drag all that shit out all the time?"

"I suppose." I stand up and brush off the back of my skirt. "I'm dining with Will at eight. I'll get ready early, and ride public transit around for a time, to muddy the trail, as the saying goes."

"We should keep eyes on you," Dolly says.

"By all means. I'll use my earbuds, as always, and you'll be in proximity, I hope. Here's the address."

"We'll manage it," Dolly says.

"You always do."

Chapter Eleven

Bits wakes up as I'm putting the finishing touches on my makeup and selecting jewelry. I'm surprised at how pleased I am with the new dress; some of it has to do with the low cost, and the fact that it's new. But it's subtly patterned in peacock feathers and goes with the heels I intend to wear, though really the entire point of a good workhorse pair of black high heels—with a stiletto in at least one heel—is that they go with just about everything.

"How dangerous do you think he is?" Bits asks through her yawn.

"I think he has the potential to be very dangerous. Coercive, perhaps, I can see him bullying me into a car or something, but not drugging me or having me shot or any of those things."

"Well that's…reassuring," Dolly says, squinting.

"Such is life," I say with a shrug, sniffing the hyacinth perfume and then applying it lightly to my wrists and the base of my neck. Put perfume where you want to be kissed, the magazines say. If my hair comes down at any point, or if Will stands behind me, the scent there will be intoxicating. "Where is the nearest bus, other than right out front?"

"Three blocks east," Bits says after a moment. "Here. New phone and earbuds. I already duped all your stuff, but you'll have to fiddle to get your settings just right again. I guess you can do that on the bus."

"I will," I say, slipping the phone onto my wrist. It doesn't fit just right with the bangles, the way the old one did, but it matches their profile pretty well. I'm certain nobody will notice but me.

"You're sure you want to do this?" Dolly's tone is softer than usual.

"It's fine. You'll be in the wings if I need you."

"Really, if that big guy in the hotel room is the only person I get to shoot, I guess we should still consider this a good job. None of us has even gotten shot at," Dolly says.

"Yet," I say with a little smile. "Let's not tempt fate."

The hotel's area of the city is full of industrial parks and mirror-faced office buildings, driverless automated vehicles, the occasional police patrol car. As I walk my three blocks to the bus station, I see the same police car four times, in fact. The fifth time, before the bus arrives, the officer slows to a stop at the curb in front of the bus station bench. I've already fixed my earbud settings, and have begun to idly search around in my saved music at a low volume, hoping to catch something with the right tempo to put me in the proper businesslike place.

"Do you need help with anything?" the officer calls, rolling his curbside window down.

"You're so kind to stop and check in on me! No, thank you, I'm just waiting on the six fifteen bus."

"I'm not sure I've ever seen somebody like you waiting at this stop," he says.

I smile, rapidly calculating what he could mean. Is he accusing me of being a prostitute? Is he just trying to flirt, but doing so very oddly? That's hardly appropriate. "It's certainly my first time at this stop."

"You came over from the hotel?"

"That's right. Having a little work retreat there."

"It's a nice place," the cop says. The radio in his dashboard mutters, and he bends his head to listen.

"He isn't a cop with a public history of doing terrible things," Bits says in my earbud. "If that helps at all."

"A little," I say softly, carefully, when I'm sure his attention is focused. "Anything else?"

"Not without a lot of dangerous digging that, at the moment, could draw far more heat than we need."

"An accident downtown might've delayed your bus," the cop says after several moments of consulting his equipment. The radio in the cop car crackles again, and then beeps a couple of times. "You take care of yourself. It can be dangerous out here alone for a woman."

"If you only knew," I say once he drives away, partly to see if Bits will laugh. Bits sort of snorts, her attention already elsewhere I'm sure.

The bus is automated and entirely empty. I pause before running my payment, and then go on with it. If the government, Russian or otherwise, hijacked an entire bus to get their hands on me, disembarking at this point will only delay the inevitable. I spend more time than I'd like on public transportation; the smells alone are enough to straighten one's hair. But I also resent paying for cabs and things, when the vast price difference could mean a new turtlescale piece, or another lipstick in my arsenal. The one I use on locks isn't my only variation on the theme.

The sidewalk is starting to speckle with rain when I get off the bus, all of the city lights blossoming dandelion halos around them. I wrap a surveillance scarf around my head and shoulders carefully, a black one this time with gold thread details and a tiny bit of fringe. I move in amongst the thin crowd and use the darkening windows to check for followers. None that I can tell, as I step into a department store. Walking straight through, the doors on the other side puts me onto a more opportune street, where I can catch another bus to ride for a few blocks.

"Looking clear," Bits says. "Except you did all that with your makeup and now it's raining."

"It's waterproof. I could go swimming like Esther Williams and be fine."

"Who?"

"Nevermind." I stop and looked in a mirror to be sure, but there isn't anything to worry about. "Time?"

"After the next bus, you should just take a cab to the restaurant."

"How are you tracking me, anyway? Or is that a silly thing to ask? You gave me this phone."

"Got it in one." This time, Bits does laugh.

"I don't suppose you have a window on my date?"

"Dolly has a vantage on the restaurant already, doesn't see any unusual activity. He isn't there yet either. The first seating is just clearing out."

"I'm surprised we're just not all linked up."

"Compartmentalization. Each of you tracks back to a different place, so we're not just a big glowing target for somebody to find."

I'm almost out of the department store when I notice a display of men's handkerchiefs. Not a major thing, but sufficient quality to catch the eye. I hesitate, go ahead and scan the code with my phone, tapping another prepaid account.

"A gift?" Bits asks once I'm back on the sidewalk.

"It's selfish to expect flowers but give nothing in return, wouldn't you say?" Literally everybody just walks around talking in this manner, though I've watched so many old movies, it still makes me self conscious sometimes. I still look around to see if anybody seems to be paying me more attention than they should, which is a difficult metric. I cultivate most aspects of myself to draw attention.

"I mean, you're not wrong."

The bus is another brief jaunt, though not solo this time. I cross the threshold for rush hour, and twenty or more people in suits are sitting or slumping in the bus seats, faces in their phones, or just staring vacantly.

I arrive at the restaurant at quarter past eight; perfectly acceptable, especially as I may have deliberately told Will the incorrect time. Second seating is at eight thirty.

"I was beginning to think you weren't coming," he says, stepping outside to meet me. He opens an umbrella, but a split second too late, and both of us get rained upon. I smile at the resulting waft of hyacinths.

"You worry too much," I say, and hand him the handkerchief box. His expression had changed just slightly when he smelled the hyacinths, and he seems entirely surprised by the flat box with its gray and white handkerchief inside.

"That's very thoughtful of you, Bristol, thank you."

"No more Chelsea?" I ask.

"I told you my name, it would have been kind to tell me yours," he says, offering his elbow. I rest my hand on it as we climb the steps to the maitre'd.

"Where did you fish up "Bristol?""

"It's what Marquis calls you," Will says. "Marquis is a very...interesting character. I don't suppose Marquis has ever been one of your suitors?"

"I hardly think that's an appropriate question for you to ask me about a dear friend. You and I have only spoken a handful of times, and you've only spoken to Marquis..."

"Just the once, to ascertain the beguiling blonde I'd met at the hotel wasn't Marquis, and to find out more about her."

"I'm quite flattered." I take a sip of water. "But I don't know anything about you, least of which if Will is your real name, or just one that you picked out of a hat to use in that hotel room."

"Is that how you chose "Chelsea?""

"It's a neighborhood in London."

"Of course." He fiddles with the items on the table in front of him, realigning the silverware after he folds the napkin in his lap, squaring the handkerchief box with the corner of the table. "Will is my real name," he says presently. Waiting people out must be one of his very best techniques. He keeps trying it out on me. "Though Bristol still isn't yours."

"No. But it's a true name, one I go by both for work and with friends." We aren't given a wine list, the glasses are simply filled. "My turn?"

"If that's how we'll play the game," Will says with a smile. I return the smile; perhaps he would relax if he thinks it was a game with rules, parameters. Boundaries he can find the edges of.

"Where are you from?"

"Virginia, born and raised."

"No accent, though." Granted, Dolly is my gold standard for this. Not all southern accents are created equal.

"No. Went to boarding school in the north, to my mother's delight and father's chagrin."

"Is she a northerner?"

"No, from Charleston." He says this as though it's all the explanation necessary, and I sort of nod, mystified. "Honestly, it's hard for me to make sense of your speech patterns," he says.

"Finishing school. Well, and some other places here and there." It's a relief that nobody seems to guess I am entirely a fraud, rags to riches, and not somebody rich who is slumming it for fun.

The waiter brings the first course, which appears to be a tiny forest built upon a piece of slate. A slow mist rolls through the trees, and the waiter lights a very small campfire on the corner of the slate. I clasp my hands and take in the little scene. The whole thing is entirely ridiculous, of course, but the workmanship is amazing.

"I'm afraid to eat it," Will says baldly.

"I know, I don't want to ruin it!"

"No, I mean I'm afraid to eat it. Like, this isn't food."

"Of course it's food. That's what, liquid nitrogen? Which probably means there's a sorbet in the middle there for us to cleanse our palates once we're done with the rest. And there's probably something we're meant to skewer and toast over the fire, so you haven't rescued me from campfire food after all." I lean forward a bit, hunting with my eyes, and then, experimentally, uproot one of the trees. It comes away easily, and the bark feels very slightly crackly.

"Well I did try." He skeptically watches me eat the tree in delicate bites. "But what is it?"

"Quail, I'd say. If it was ortolan we'd have been instructed to cover our faces."

Will selects his own tree and copies my approach, balancing it on his fork over the fire before chewing thoughtfully. "You probably already know this, but you're the most cultured person I've ever sat down with."

"I suspected, but it's still nice to hear." I pull another tree. The sorbet is visible now, and we must get to it soon. "Your turn."

"You came here alone tonight?" he asks. I arch a brow at him, look around. "I know you got here alone. I'm asking if your charming friend from the hotel is waiting outside. Or a sniper."

"The windows in this room aren't real, just elaborate light fixtures. Didn't you notice when we were outside?" I spoon up some of the sorbet. Lemongrass, I think.

"You understand, this isn't how interviews normally go. Typically I ask the questions, make the demands, and you act agreeably."

"The upset of the power balance is throwing you, it's natural. And can you really say I'm not acting agreeably?"

"It happens to everybody," Bits murmurs in my ear, and I finish my glass of wine to stave off the giggles. Will has reached the sorbet as well and doesn't seem to notice, and then the waiter puts the fire out and whisks away the slate and wine glasses.

"I wonder what they'll bring us next," Will says. "I've never gone to a restaurant where I didn't tell them what I wanted." I give him a particular smile, and he laughs. "That's it, the power balance thing again. This entire day, week, whatever, is an object lesson. I'm sure I'm really growing as a person."

"At least you enjoy your work," I say as a bowl is set in front of each of us. It looks like a regular bowl of soup, coconut milk with edible flowers, and is almost a disappointment after the majesty of the misty forest. "This is some of the best coconut milk soup I've ever had," I say after a moment, regretting my doubts.

"Even when you were in Thailand?"

"Oh, I've never been to Thailand," I say dismissively. "Hong Kong, though. Did you know, in Hong Kong, there are places that are a combination of gigantic swimming pools and fishing holes, where you can go any hour of the day or night to rent a pole and go fishing? You can have the fish cooked up if you want, if you catch something. You see gangsters there in the middle of the night. They need to relax too, if you can imagine."

"I did not know you could do that in Hong Kong. Or anywhere else for that matter, except an actual natural body of water. Gangsters, you say?"

"Gangsters, young professionals, everybody really. But the people who go in the middle of the night aren't typically law abiding locals."

"And how would you know?"

"I went to see the gangsters, of course." I saw it on a travel show that was actually more about food, but was also very culturally informing indeed.

"Of course."

"He's really never going to get to it," Dolly says in wonder. I'd missed her connecting. "He's really just going to treat this like a date the entire evening. Next time, I get to seduce the charming young man of the story." Bits laughs.

The next course is a plate of fish for each of us that seems entirely whole, head and fins and all. I stare at it blankly for a moment, distracted by the voices in my ears. I look up at Will. "I'm sorry, I didn't quite catch that."

"I said I do enjoy my work. Though I'm one of the youngest in the regional branch, so I'm constantly having to prove that I'm not just some punk kid who lucked into a good assignment."

"Does that mean the other day was very embarrassing for you? I am sorry."

"Not as embarrassing for me as it was for the gorilla at the door, anyway."

"Was he one of yours?"

"He was the courier's hired muscle. He just happens to be local talent." Will pauses, carefully dismantling his fish. It appears it was just cunningly put back together, which is a relief. The entire head is a rebuilding of other materials, not just an intact fish skull with eyes and everything. "But yes, he was ours."

"And here you are the, what, investigative lead? This is your first time on lead, isn't it?" I rest my chin in my hands and gaze at him. "That is dreadfully exciting."

"I'm glad you think so," Will says drily. "But we haven't really made much progress here."

"We're getting to know each other. We're having excellent food, or an excellent food experience, anyway. I'm certain you can be reasonably worked with. You have an idea of what you're after, I'm sure?"

"A few things, yeah." He fiddles with the handkerchief box again. I test myself, my eye for these things, looking at his tie bar; it does seem similar to the one he wore at the hotel, if not the same one. There's no reason to believe he isn't also wearing earbuds. When he pauses, maybe he's listening to his team members. What a farce this is.

"Well, what are you prepared to offer?"

"See, Marquis said to watch for a particular look in your eyes. He—"

"They," I interrupt.

"What?"

"They. Marquis uses the pronoun they. Marquis is not a he. Or a she."

Will recovers sooner than I expected. "They said that the look would be like that hard glitter when morning sun is on ocean waves, and I thought they were just being poetic, because to me it seems impossible to not be infatuated with you after even a brief meeting, but it's there now. That look."

"Poetics can still be truthful."

"So I see. And I believe Marquis was in a position to feel very truthful."

They want to make a deal. A flutter of unease, and I frown and shift in my chair. "Where is Marquis?"

"Marquis is safe. What do you take us for?"

"It isn't as though all of the masks are off, even when the gloves are, yes?"

"Yes." Will studies me for a long moment, and the waiter takes the fish away, mostly uneaten. "I'm not threatening you, or your friends. What we are discussing is larger than the individuals involved here. I imagine you became involved because you anticipated a payday. Well, we are prepared to pay. We just need to know the package is as intact as possible, all the pieces recoverable."

"All the pieces are recoverable," I say, hoping Bits won't prove me wrong. Silence in the earbuds.

"That's very good to know." The waiter sets glossy black spheres in front of each of us, and small pourable tureens of what seem to be hot fudge. "So then we can arrange..."

Will keeps talking, but Dolly is in my ears, louder than before, brisk, businesslike. "We've got a chopper incoming, which may or may not have to do with us, but the SUV's that all pulled up out front are definitely coming in there for one of you. Or both. They are *not* friendlies, they are openly carrying weapons. AR-15's looks like. I can engage, but there are too many for me to take all of them cleanly. This ain't exactly the best sniper roost I've ever had."

I keep my eyes on the dessert, picking up the hot chocolate tureen and pouring it over the black sphere. The blackness is darker chocolate, and it melts slowly away, displaying another garden scene within, this one including spun sugar lilies.

"They don't seem to be on Will's side," Bits says. "Their chatter isn't in English, and what I assume to be his chatter is. There's another radio network that's got personnel scrambling, and I assume that's whoever Will set up to be nearby. Both of you, take your exits. Now. Go."

I stand abruptly, chair knocking back, teetering on two legs, and then coming to rest again. I look at Will, who has also risen. Calculate. "Come with me," I say, and head towards the back of the restaurant, where I'd seen the holographic flicker of an exit sign when we came in.

"What the hell?"

"Trust me." I call over my shoulder, without turning. Could I hear heavy boots in the entryway, or was I just anticipating them? The creak of buckles on ripstop gun straps, the short slap of combat knife sheaths against a thigh or the small of a back. I leave the dining room rapidly, not running, and not all of the diners even bothered to look. Is Will behind me? He is if he's smart.

I turn the corner and there's the exit sign, across from doors to the kitchen, and I'm there in six steps, each one quicker than the last, high heels a staccato rhythm on the hardwood. Yes, those are his shiny shoes behind me. I slap my hands onto the emergency bar and a klaxon sounds throughout the building. LEDs flash at various emergency stations, and voices of diners begin to raise, even before I hear the front door explode inward in what has to be a cloud of splinters. It's a real wooden door.

We clatter down a concrete stairwell, and exit into a non-descript alley. I glance back briefly, past Will, to see if anybody else chose this exit as well. Even at this distance, there are raised voices, questioning, and other louder voices which are more strident, demanding, and I freeze for a split second when I hear a gun go off. I really need to become less gun shy.

Then Will has his arm across the small of my back and is urging me down the alleyway. There's a brief comedic moment where both Will's getaway car and mine are both there waiting. "Follow us," Will says finally. I nod, sliding into the backseat. No more gunfire behind us, I don't know if that's good or bad.

"You heard?"

"Yeah, we'll follow," Dolly says, and we drive off into the night.

Chapter Twelve

"So I hope this is the right choice," Bits says, holding the VR visor to her face; something seems to have happened to the strap.

"Well, they're not the ones shootin' at us," Dolly growls. There's a tear in her shirt and her ponytail is half fallen out, but she seems unhurt.

"I'm confident this is the better outcome," I offer.

"Oh, that's what you got outta you two making moon eyes at each other for three courses? Because it didn't seem like you were doing anything useful, from what I could hear."

"Moon eyes?"

Dolly makes a noise of disgust and waves her hands. "You know what I mean."

"Moon eyes," I say again. "Bits?"

"She isn't wrong," Bits says after a moment, picking her head up. The visor is still switched on, and colors play across Bits's face from below. "They didn't shut down their systems at all, and it looks like they called in cavalry to handle whoever it was that showed up in the SUVs. One agent was shot before they made it to their vehicles, but is stable. We're going to an undisclosed location, of course, but it seems like it might be on the industrial end of the docks."

"This is just really weird," Dolly says. "Why all that old bullshit about the eggs and submarines and Anastasia and stuff?"

"If an assumed lost Fabergé egg were to enter the market, the world would be in a clamor. Those items haven't been seen in more than a hundred years. It would be like if somebody knocked out an old wall in a coldwater flat in Liverpool and realized that the amber room was hidden behind it." I try to sound casual about it, but really, if I were to come into possession of something like a lost Fabergé egg, it would become the thing I was most private about in my life, a tiny jeweled thing which I could admire for my own pleasure and never tell anybody about. I hope that's the kind of person whose care those lost eggs have been in. I hope they're in a quiet room with drawn curtains and soft light to play off the facets of the jewels, and that delicate and caring hands occasionally open them to look at the marvelous treasure inside. I ache for such an opportunity.

"The amber room?" Dolly asks.

"Just another one of those magnificent things lost because of Nazis or war or both," I say.

Bits sighs, and then the brake lights ahead of us flash, flash again, and the car makes a sharp left without signaling. "What's our game plan going in here?" she asks, drumming her fingers on her knee.

"We want to be paid, we want to be safe, and we want our freedom," I say. "The same things we always want. Just because we think we might be dealing with actual big shot governmental good guys, or less-bad guys, does not change that in the slightest."

"There are times butter wouldn't melt in your mouth," Dolly says, but seems to intend it as a compliment.

"It's the only way to get by, sometimes. I assume I'll do the most talking?"

"Sure, so long as you get to the point, instead of endless small talk," Dolly says. We follow the car through a barbed wire topped chain link fence, onto what seems to be an abandoned shipping yard, containers piled high in the darkness, a few absolutely ancient arc sodium lights standing sentry at the perimeters.

We make the final turn, around one of the piles of shipping containers, and then it's searingly bright, big LEDs set up underneath a canopy that hides their light in a way I don't quite understand, but Bits probably will. There's big boats of indeterminate type nearby, and a few squat buildings, and I assume most of it is scenery to camouflage whatever the actual operation here is.

Dolly whistles aimlessly as we park and get out of the car, just a repeating run of notes, and I think about asking her to stop, and then don't. Dolly and Bits are both in riot gear, which is both amusing and perhaps appropriate; as I walk ahead and they come in on my flanks. They almost seem like bodyguards, though I sincerely hope none of this will come to that.

I wonder where Bits and Dolly have stowed the diamonds. I have every faith that while I was making my way across town, they were making sure the diamonds were someplace safe. It's actually very smart for me to not know that location just now. I can only assume Bits copied the files and has that encrypted and squirreled away in her systems somewhere.

Will comes to meet us. He left his umbrella at the restaurant, but I'd never even properly set my purse down. He does, however, have the handkerchief box, and that tiny thing makes my smile that much brighter "We approach the command center?" I ask.

"It's this way. This is all of you?" He looks at Dolly, then at Bits, then back to Dolly. "You did the hotel room amazingly clean," he says.

"I do take pride in my work," she says dryly, leaning into her drawl.

"And this is...technology and equipment?" Will looks at Bits again.

"You got it."

"Interesting. Very interesting. We've had a few days to speculate. But come on."

"Just to be clear, Will, are we under arrest?"

"What? No. You're free to leave any time you'd like. Though after what just happened I don't know why you might want to."

"I'm not sure why we'd want to stay. We still don't know who you are."

"That's right, that's true, I'm sorry. Come on." The other men in suits are out of the car, also stoic in the rain, but they just watch Will carry on. He leads us into a building practically in the water. I wonder when the nearest boat left shore last, and whether it ever will again. Everything within sight is weeping rust, and the way that boat's deck slumps towards the waterline, it seems like another prop, like more set dressing.

More people in black suits, men and women, are inside the first door Will opens, and he gestures us through. No obvious guns, but I pick out holsters as we breeze through. There are innumerable screens in the room. Hastily dimmed wall displays; tablets set on tables; on every agent's wrist, phones. They aren't all standing at attention, exactly, but they aren't busy at work either. They watch us cross the room.

The next room has wood paneling and no windows, as though a board room was transported from a skyscraper to this rundown building. I settle myself in the cushy chair at the head of the table, rocking back in it a little. Dolly and Bits follow my lead, and Dolly kicks her feet up onto the table with a grin. "Y'know, I've always wanted to do that in a place like this," she says.

"By all means, make yourself comfortable," Will says, not even hiding his smile. Heaven help him if he thinks we're *cute*. Dolly will eat his entrails.

"Your boyfriend is very nice, Bristles," Dolly says, and I smile at the little bit of pink that creeps above Will's collar.

"So what are we going to talk about, William?" I ask. Bits is working on her headset strap.

"Just Will," he says.

"I'm almost disappointed, but that's fascinating."

"Says the woman who hasn't told me her real name."

I wave my hand. "It's boring, I promise you."

"I'm sure."

"No, really. Names have a certain meaning and feeling. As children, we're named like puppies pulled from a cardboard box; it isn't necessarily going to bear the most cosmic weight."

"Well this took a turn," Dolly says, pivoting her chair towards Bits, who's holding the visor to her face again. She makes a distant noise of assent.

"We should get back on track," Will says. "I don't want your friends to get bored."

"We're bored already," Dolly says with a wink, and I sigh.

"Yes, business is business," I say.

"I'm glad you agree." Will stands behind the seat at the foot of the table, leaning his elbows on the back. "Now that we see what the other side is willing to do, can we cut to the chase?"

"Of course. I do apologize that you don't enjoy the banter. It's one of my few recreations."

Dolly sighs loudly and puts her boots up on the table again.

"Right. So. Where are the diamonds?"

"They're safe."

"They're easily recoverable?"

"More or less," Bits mutters, and at first I'm not sure Will hears her, but he bows his head slightly and rubs the back of his neck.

"That's good, I guess. And you've still got all of them? Haven't broken up the lot, sold or traded any?"

"We have them all," I say. It seems better for our safety that Will and his people don't know we're aware of the data. "They seemed more valuable as a set."

"That's more or less correct," he says. "Mrs. Carter would've been happy to carry that set away for herself. Maybe set it in a tiara or something."

"Mrs. Carter seems past tiara wearing age," I say. "Unless she's the leader of a small island nation that she rules with an iron fist in a velvet glove."

"She has a compound, anyway," Will says, perhaps a bit hastily. I smile, and wait. "Mrs. Carter, though, was working for foreign interests. She was a known authority to tap for this diamond sale. It would probably not surprise you to learn that the only reason they were for sale is that they were stolen from their rightful owners."

"And you intend to return them to their rightful owners?" I ask, tilting my head just a bit.

"Well, no." He clears his throat, then pulls out the chair and sits, still seeming a bit awkward. "No, the rightful owners are not to be considered allies."

"Ergo, Mrs. Carter is also not an ally."

"Correct. The purpose of the sale was to show off, ultimately. Espionage right under our noses. The seller, Richard, was an independent agent. He was paid handsomely, and in charge of the diamonds simply for his authority in the field."

"What a strange setup," I say.

"People like the ceremony of it. And figure nothing can happen, of course." Will muses on that for a moment. "Anyway. I don't know who you intended to sell the diamonds to, or if you tried already, but we are prepared to offer you each a comfortable sum in exchange for bringing them to us."

"I'm sorry, but why are they so important?" I ask. "Other than being remarkable stones."

Will clears his throat, frowning just a little bit. "Their base monetary value is a factor, of course. Nobody likes losing money."

"That's true, very true. And?"

"You know I can't fully disclose here," he says.

"Ah, girls, the diamonds have secrets," I say.

Dolly takes her boots off the table. "Can I smoke in here or what?" she asks.

"Go ahead," Will says.

Bits briefly pushes the VR headset up on top of her head. "You just told us they're more than they seem. This only increases the value," she says.

"Indeed." I raise an eyebrow at Will. "Last chance, I suppose, before we start writing figures on napkins. Or handkerchiefs, I suppose, as the room seems sorely lacking in a bar. Anything else?"

"There's nothing else you need to know about the diamonds," Will says evenly, but his frown, the unhappy quirk of his lips, that's the tell.

"All right, then. Get out your pen."

"Is this really necessary?" Will asks. He pulls a pen from the breast pocket of his very nice suit, and opens the handkerchief box.

"Are you hurt because you thought I got you a nice present for the sake of it?" I ask.

"No, I'm not—"

"We've got incoming," Bits says abruptly.

"How do you—" Will starts

"Hush. Bits, darling, what kind of incoming? We're in a port, there's a certain amount of traffic to be expected."

"A line of cars coming down the road we just took, in addition to one boat and something in the air, which might just be drones and not a chopper."

Will puts a hand to his ear, so yes, of course he has earbuds. He says, "It isn't a chopper, you're correct. Go out this door please."

"You've provided for this, one might assume?" I ask.

"Yes, but you're not going to want to walk on the decking in those heels," Will says.

"Everybody is so damned worried about my shoes."

Will holds the door impatiently. Dolly's already down the hallway as I pull my heels off and slip into a pair of folded leather ballet slippers from my purse.

The blandly painted passageway is yellow-lit, getting darker as Will leads us down several flights of stairs. Bits keeps her headset on and her hand on Dolly's back for guidance, keeping electronic tabs on whoever the interlopers are.

Surrounded by our breathing and footfalls, my eyes strain in the close darkness for light, for anything at all. It's dark enough and for long enough that I begin to see colors in the dark, like old-fashioned television static, and imagine shadows moving towards us, even though nobody else reacts to them. I was never afraid of the dark as a child, and it feels foolish to suddenly have that kind of fear now, but this is a profound and complete darkness that I was unprepared for. I try to to take stock, to set my focus on something other than the yawning emptiness around me. Dolly must have some kind of night vision in her augmented contact lenses and Will brought us here so decisively he must have something guiding him as well, so I'm the only one at the disadvantage, a position I sorely resent. I put my hand out straight, and encounter the smooth-rough fabric of Will's coat, still slightly damp from the rain, and the movement brings a waft of the hyacinth perfume to my nostrils.

"Watch your eyes," Will says just before opening a door into a hallway made out of white light.

"Where are we going?" It seems prudent to ask.

"There's a sub we can take. It's only a matter of time before the opposition is right here with us."

"A sub? Isn't this getting a little ridiculous?"

"This is already ridiculous," Dolly mutters. She never even got the chance to put her e cigarette away.

"They've engaged with your people upstairs," Bits says. "Though my connection is getting spotty." She pushes the VR visor up again and blinks at us.

"Communications from down here are typically bad," Will says. "And I guess that depends on your threshold for the ridiculous. I'll just ask again straight out, because we don't have time for anything else, do you have the diamonds with you?"

"Of course not. Why would we bring our only bargaining chip into a completely unknown scenario?"

"Right, excuse me."

The next set of doors are heavy steel and swing shut behind us with an ominous hollow bang, and here the concrete floor extends into walkways and gratings and water that smelled slightly brackish. Will slaps an honest to goodness big red button on the wall, and a klaxon sounds.

"Is that necessary or simply for effect?" I ask.

"Six of one, half dozen of the other," Will says. He gestures us towards one of the walkways, where the water boils up white and then a submarine breaks the surface, just like in all the movies. "Your chariot."

"And where are we going?" I ask again.

"Now this time, that's classified. We won't stay there long, you aren't prisoners, nobody's under arrest. We just need to assess and regroup. Someplace safe." Distant thumping briefly draws his attention, and a muscle in Dolly's jaw twitches. Water finishes pouring off the top of the sub, which lines up with the walkway. The hatch on top opens.

"Is this manned or remotely operated?" Bits asks.

"Manned. We'll see them once we're underway." We walk across the damp decking on top of the sub, and there's a ladder down the hatch. It really is a good thing that I keep flats in my purse, but for once in my life, I do feel the lack of riot gear.

Chapter Thirteen

Will briefly goes out of sight, presumably to converse with the submarine operators, and then leads us to a narrow galley with a small lounge. There's a couch, and table, and chairs, all just slightly too small for comfort. "I don't suppose anybody's hungry," he says. I shake my head.

"I could eat," Dolly says with a shrug.

"I'll see what I can do to make that happen." He rummages behind a partition.

Bits stows the headset. "I wonder if the car's all right," she says.

"Did you pack everything from the hotel into it before you left?" I ask.

"Nah, just some essentials, key items," Dolly says. "We didn't want to touch any of your stuff."

I stare at her. "So you just...left it? To be thrown out?"

"We're paid through the end of the week," Bits says. "It'll be there"

Will comes back with an armful of MRE's. "It isn't gourmet, but it'll be edible, anyway."

"I think our definitions of edible—" I begin, and Dolly interrupts me.

"It'll be calories, is what you mean," she says, taking one. "These don't require much explanation. They're always better with hot sauce, of course."

"I'm getting used to the fact that I'll probably never have a grasp of what you three know." Will shakes his head and sits down.

"Just think of it as a good way to round out your field experience." Dolly pulls the heat tab on one of the cans. "Complacency is dangerous."

"You're not wrong." Will examines the labels on a couple of the MREs, then pulls one open. "The gourmet experience was also a new one. I didn't actually go to that restaurant in Chicago, I just watched one of those chef shows," he says to me, a little apologetically.

"It isn't for everybody," I say.

Dolly laughs. "It isn't for people who are actually hungry."

"Appetites vary," I say with a sniff. "But, shall we continue our discussion? I think we were reaching figures."

"I've had word that we're supposed to hold off on that," Will says. "Other parties would like to be present."

"Oh? And after we've established such a magnificent rapport! What a shame."

"I'm sure they have their reasons." His neck does not redden. "It'll be fine. We'll be safe, we'll get a greater understanding of who our enemies are and what they're willing to do. Things will progress."

"If you say so." I cross my legs. The sub is very echoey, and clangy. Bits seems at loose ends without technology to reach for. "They seem willing to do quite a lot."

"Well. We'll also assess if both attacks came from the same party. All three attacks, if we include the raid on the arcade the other night."

"That was so stupid," Bits says. "We should never have made a mistake like that."

"You can't think of everything," I say, and Bits shakes her head.

"Something like that I absolutely should have."

"The fact that I could still call Bristol saved you some trouble," Will says.

"And the fact that you were able to call her is why we had trouble to begin with. Don't just say things to make me feel better when you don't even know me."

"Duly noted," Will says with an embarrassed smile.

"Thank you."

"Welcome to your view of the other side," Dolly says with a grin, moving on to another packet from her MRE. "Here's hoping it's educational."

"Oh, it already has been," Will says, with a brief glance in my direction.

"We're so pleased to have been a help to you and your organization," I say with a smile. "Is our secure and undisclosed location very far?"

"Not much longer." He checks his watch. "Another half hour, maybe?"

"And then we'll have our own fresh and educational view of your side of things."

"I hadn't thought of it that way." Will in fact seems slightly alarmed. I try to mentally construct a very short description of what I think our attribution in the case file would be, as if I know how case files are worded. A group of thieves? A group of well equipped thieves? A group of capable thieves? The thieves part has to stick, obviously. We robbed a great deal of diamonds from a group of wealthy and powerful people. For a brief moment, I again allow myself to think of how it would be to have one of those Fabergé eggs in my hands. Or just that blue diamond again.

Dolly and Will are finished with their MRE's by the time a tone sounds through the overhead speakers, and a woman comes on, saying "We're in the final approach."

"Finally," Dolly says, and I reapply my lipstick.

"Who will we be meeting here?" I ask Will.

"Mr. Harding is the lead here," he says after a moment's hesitation.

"Mr. Harding. Good to know, thank you. Is there anything else I should know about Mr. Harding?"

"I'm not going to brief you on my boss," he says with a disbelieving laugh.

I cap my lipstick and dropped it back into my purse with a shrug. "You can't blame a girl for trying."

He's about to comment, but then there's a rising sensation, and a little jolt.

"I feel as though we're approaching a Bond villain's lair," I say as we follow Will out of the galley and back to the hatch.

"We're the good guys," Will says.

"Everybody thinks they're the good guys." And then the hatch overhead opens, and more yellow light pours in.

We climb out of the sub and into another underground area, this one far less concrete bunker and far more natural cave. A tall man in a suit much like Will's waits for us on dry land. "Cut it close, didn't you?" he asks Will.

Will glances at Bits briefly before answering. "It turned out alright."

"Be that as it may..." His gaze rakes over Bits and Dolly in their riot gear, lingers on me in my date night dress. "You ladies have caused quite the commotion."

"It's a habit we've cultivated," I say. "Though we realized a little late that we were in quite a more complicated situation than we'd intended."

"Yes. It's interesting that you realized that before things got too far out of hand," Harding scowls. "It's almost embarrassing that this meeting took so long."

"We're used to being underestimated," I say smoothly. "And it's no fault of Will's that we anticipated contact. Really, what happened is our initial diamond buyer decided he wasn't going to touch the stones, which was unusual to say the least. And when we withdrew to regroup, things started to go a bit pear shaped."

"A pretty story, but there's more to it," Mr. Harding says.

"Why, of course there is. But are we going to stand about in a submarine dock all evening?"

He scowls again, for longer, then looks at Will. "This is your responsibility," he says, and turns.

We follow them into extremely dull-looking office quarters. We pause at a reception window and Mr. Harding berates the just-out-of-sight staffer for a few moments. I take the time to swap back to my high heels, folding the ballet slippers again and rolling them up in a spare handkerchief as an extra precaution against moisture.

The door buzzes and Mr. Harding stands back to let us through, Will taking the lead. He notices the noise of my heels on the tiled floor immediately, and if anything, his scowl abates just a little bit. I pat my hair briefly; my hair pins are still in place.

As we walk, Bits looks at door frames, corners, framed pictures. I'm not certain what she's checking for, but it's more than possible that Bits is also wearing augmented contact lenses. Or did Bits have the corneal augmentation surgery? She certainly didn't tell me about it. The notion of layering contacts with a headset makes me feel delicately nauseous; I'd put on a VR headset once in my life and fallen over immediately, a nosebleed ensuing. Bits is the one who inhabits that role, living a virtual life along with a real one.

"If you ladies wouldn't mind using this room while we debrief Will here, we'll be with you in just a little while. There are some vending machines, coded open access. If you need anything else, just knock on the door." Mr. Harding smiles then, a very trained and necessary smile, and I smile back warmly.

"That would be just fine, Mr. Harding, thank you."

The room seems to be an employee lounge, with a table and straight backed chairs in one end where the vending machines are, and a couch and more comfortable cushioned chairs taking up the rest of the space. There is a sparsely populated bookshelf, which seems to be made up mostly of cheap reprint paperbacks and some augmented magazines, the type with holo ads and video accompaniment to some articles, considerably less cheap.

"How does it look, Bits?" I ask, once the door is closed. She's already shoved the headset onto her face. I'm not sure when she fixed the strap.

"Pretty secure," Bits says. "We're probably not going to get ambushed here. Even if they tried, it would be a poor prospect. No fortress is impregnable or whatever, but this one is pretty good. I've read about facilities like it, dark place on the map. They're probably listening to us here—so hi guys—but it seems safe enough. Now to hope that Will makes good on his promise that we're safe, not under arrest, and that we will be worked with on this to recover those diamonds they want so badly."

"Good. So no surprises either."

"Not really."

By the time Mr. Harding comes back, Bits and Dolly are both asleep. Or Bits is still doing mysterious tech things, there's no real way for me to tell the difference without trying to talk to her. I spend the time trying to make sure my thoughts are in order.

Mr. Harding walks into the room and seems briefly thrown off that I sit serenely waiting for him, hands folded, ankles crossed. "I'm sorry, that took longer than intended."

"Oh, it isn't a worry at all," I say. "This space is quite relaxing."

"I'm glad you think so." He sits at the end of the couch nearest my chair. "Do I need to address all three of you?"

"I've been authorized to speak for the group. It's what Will and I were working towards over dinner, after all."

"Yes, quite." Mr. Harding clears his throat. "Quite the resourceful trio, aren't you? I suppose it isn't so unusual, in this day and age. But remarkable, yes."

"Well thank you very much." I smile. And I wait.

"As I understand it, you and Will were in fact at the point of coming to terms?" Mr. Harding seems to hesitate a bit each time he says Will's name, as though he in fact means to say Agent something instead, or Mr. something.

"We were, I think."

"I see. I'm authorized to offer half a million dollars for each of you, in the manner of your choosing. We can give you cash, though that'll make the boys in accounting shit their pants, the boys in security feel even worse, thinking of the suitcases just on the street while you choose banks or sew it up into mattresses or whatever else you intend to do with it."

"Half a million each?" I repeat. "That is rather generous."

"We think so, and we can get it to you as soon as—"

"I think it sort of seems to be worth more than the stones intrinsic value, wouldn't you say?" I ask idly.

"Why would you say that?"

"I did have a chance to look at them in the hotel room, after all, with the grading instruments present. Of course, the blue stone is its own beast."

"Exactly, the blue stone," Mr. Harding says. "I don't know very much about it, honestly. Me, I can't see the use for shiny things that seem to exist for the purpose of being shiny. I prefer useful things."

"Well, there are industrial uses for diamonds," I say. "But they're different stones entirely from the ones we're discussing."

"Very different, I'd think." Mr. Harding considers me a moment. He clearly thought I would fall all over myself accepting his initial offer. "What's your counter request, then?"

"I'd say a million each, for the sake of argument. Otherwise, I'd simply suspect we were being fleeced out of ignorance."

"A million each." Harding nods his head as he processes this. "That would be enough for you to retire on, live out the rest of your life, if you invested it responsibly."

"Or went to a country with a far lower cost of living," I say, thinking of places where the desert air meets the sea air. "I don't know about Bits and Dolly's goals necessarily, but personally, I'm averse to being shot at and pursued. The sooner I can normalize my situation, the better."

"I'm not sure many people prefer to be shot at, Miss."

"Bristol."

"Miss Bristol. I understand, your current situation is uncomfortable. You stepped into an unexpected arena, and there are forces at work here that not everybody is prepared to deal with. It's admirable you ladies avoided your pursuers so adeptly."

"We are quite the team," I agree. "Additionally, I want to make sure our amnesty is on paper and in your systems, signed and notarized by whoever necessary. We had no political intent in this action, and while obviously stealing in general is illegal, and stealing diamonds quite on a grand scale, we arguably kept the stones out of the incorrect hands until your organization had the time to regroup and liaise with us properly."

Another pause. "I'm sure that can be arranged," he says. Either I'm just shocking him time and again, which is hard to imagine, or he has some friends in his ears. I should always assume there are eavesdroppers, and speak accordingly.

"I think that's one of the most desirable parts of the deal," I say. "Will assured us we were neither arrested nor detained, and our freedom is very important to us, especially in the light of the payment agreement which I should hope we will reach."

"So money, your freedom, and freedom from prosecution on this particular event. Do I have it straight?"

"You do." I think furiously to see if I've forgotten anything else, but we'd meant to keep it as simple as possible.

"The amnesty would, I should hope, make it so our legal identities and passports and such function as expected, with no holds or hangups?"

"I should hope," Mr. Harding agrees. "An especially important detail, were one to retire to a foreign shore."

"The expat life is just so glamorous some places."

"I've heard that. Not for me, I love my country. But there's an appeal. Lower prices, carefree beaches, that kind of thing."

"I think we understand one another, Mr. Harding."

"You understand I need to run this past my superiors," he says. "Double the total amount, plus all the red tape with your amnesty."

"Oh, I understand. But, it isn't exactly as though we're going anywhere, is it?" I ask, gesturing at the lounge with a little laugh. Perhaps I ought to have asked for more.

"Not at the moment, anyway. You might want to get some sleep as well."

"Perhaps I will, though I do prefer a bed to other sorts of furniture. It's funny, sleeping in strange places doesn't bother me, but I do love my creature comforts."

"My wife, she can't sleep anywhere but at home. So she claims. Every time we're in a hotel, she goes on and on about this or that. As far as I can tell, she's sawing lumber, but she always says she couldn't sleep, gets a crick in her neck, all that."

"How dreadful for her."

"Yeah. For her." This time Mr. Harding laughs. Then he stands up, buttons his single button suit coat, and offers me his hand. I take it and shake firmly. "I'll talk to you in the morning. I'll send Will back here so you have a familiar face."

"It's most appreciated, Mr. Harding. How long do you think we'll be here?"

"It's hard to say. We appreciate your patience, of course."

"Of course," I say, my smile never slipping. How tiresome.

"Now have a good night. We're safe here."

It makes sense to be obsessed with safety, but making promises like that is the best way to test fate. There's no way to know everything, to track all the factors. You just make educated guesses and fling yourself into life's wayward currents. I give a little jump at the knock at the door, and then Will softly calls, "It's me, can I come in?"

I cross the room and pull open the door. "Afraid to find us in some level of indecency?"

"It's just polite," he says, and then I notice the folding cots on wheels in the hall next to him.

"Oh, you clever darling!"

"I did. Though you're probably the only one it bothers."

"Yes, I much prefer something resembling a real bed."

Will wheels the cots in, positions one and unfolds it for me. It's already up with sheets, and a folded scratchy green wool blanket. "Army issue, I'm sorry about that. They do utility, not comfort."

"It's fine, I'm sure." I slip my heels off and line them up next to the head of the bed with my purse, pull the pins from my hair. I take a moment to peel away the false eyelashes and swipe at my face with a makeup removal cloth from my purse, peering into my compact mirror to make sure I get it all. "I'm so dreadfully tired that I won't notice to complain."

"I'll be right here if you need anything," he says, browsing the sparse bookcase. He takes one of the magazines and sits at the table.

I curl up on my side, hands pillowed under my cheek. For a folding army issue cot, it's more comfortable than I might have expected, and I fall lightly and comfortably asleep to the scratch of Will paging through the magazine, tiny holo sounds occasionally reaching my ears.

Chapter Fourteen

It isn't often that I wake without some natural light in the morning, and it's disorienting. Will still sits at the table, his tie pulled loose. Dolly's there with him, working through another MRE, one of the pulp paperbacks propped in front of her. Bits is still in much the same position on the couch, with her VR headset on.

"I had hoped for a hot breakfast," I say, sitting up and stretching my arms.

"There might yet be hope for that," Will says.

"I bullied him into getting me this, I was starving."

"You must be, to eat those."

"Aw, they aren't so bad. Don't have to worry about it spoiling like fresh food, or anything getting into it. Sealed and shelf stable. Not terribly interesting, but a little hot sauce goes a long way."

"I always wondered about that little vial on your keychain. I always just assumed it was cyanide, in case we were ever captured." I slip into my heels yet again; the dress seems remarkably unwrinkled.

"Nah, the cyanide is in one of my molar replacements," Dolly says with a crooked grin, then drains the last of her coffee.

"So what's our plan for the day?" I ask. "Will we have another handler? Or will we at least be directed to a more amusing holding room while you men stomp out there and save the world?"

"You're stuck with me for now," Will says.

I wonder how long Mr. Harding will keep us waiting, if he'll try that tactic again, but then the PA system crackles and a detached female voice says, "Will Scarlet and guests, please report to conference area D." Bits gives a start and pulls her headset off.

"Shall we?" Will asks, finishing his coffee and standing.

"When *will* they let you sleep?" I ask. "I would have thought it was preferable to have you well-rested, reflexes and judgement intact."

"I'll sleep when I'm dead," he says. I have a terrible shiver of foreboding. "Hey. I keep telling you, we're safe here." Will looks as though he wants to take my hand, or put an arm around me, but he does neither.

"Ever hear the saying whistling past a graveyard?" Dolly asks, when I seem disinclined to answer, a rarity in all of our association together, to be sure.

"Yeah, why?" Will puts their books back on the shelf.

"Just thought it might apply here. Come on, let's not keep people waitin.'"

"I'm afraid they will have to wait, I absolutely must step into the ladies' room and fix myself before we have any sort of business meeting."

"You look fine," Will says, and I look at him, smiling pleasantly, until he sighs. "It's along the way."

There are numerous unmarked doors we pass along the way, and then the stereotypical pair of restroom doors, male and female. No gender neutral bathrooms in this organization.

We girls go in with no comment to one another, leaving Will to linger in the hall. I lay paper towels out on the counter, though it does appear to be a very clean facility, and pull my little travel makeup kit from my purse. I'm done nearly before Bits and Dolly are, and as an afterthought, I use the barest whisper of a spritz of the hyacinth perfume, before packing everything back up and hanging my purse in the crook of my arm again.

"It's like magic," Dolly says. She on occasion does her make-up with what is essentially a black crayon, but is very casual about it either way.

"I could teach you," I say, as always, and as always Dolly just laughs and shakes her head.

We rejoin Will, and after some more walking, reach another generic conference room. I am becoming inured to the fact that the meeting places with this organization will not, in fact, have alcohol available. But what really grabs my attention is the presence in the room besides Mr. Harding; Marquis.

"You wicked man, you didn't tell me Marquis would be here," I say, leaving it up to Mr. Harding and Will to decide who I am addressing.

I close the distance with three swift steps and Marquis catches me by the arms before I can embrace them, staring into my face. "I was so worried," they say. "You just disappeared. You just left me."

"I'm so sorry about everything," I say. Oh they're angry at me. They have every right to be so very angry with me. "I was worried about you too, but I just couldn't message you, we were barely staying ahead of—"

"I've been here since the night Will called you," Marquis says. "They wouldn't tell me anything."

"I'm so sorry," I say again. I'd hoped for a happier reunion than this, especially in front of strangers. "Are you okay?"

They shrug and let go of my arms. "Mostly bored and frustrated. Worried sick. But you look just fine. New dress?"

"I hate to interrupt the reunion, but we're going to have a person from financials in here, a notary, and another operations supervisor. Yes, before you ask, this conversation is being watched and recorded, to make sure we're making the deals we said we would. It protects all of us. Do you feel properly apprised of what the plan is moving forward?"

"Yeah, sounds great," Dolly says. She's already planted herself in one of the chairs. "We heard the recording of last night's conversation, what you an' Bristol hashed out seems just fine. Is Marquis gettin' cut into all of this?"

"Marquis has made their own arrangements," Mr. Harding says. "We'll move you to what we hope are more pleasing or entertaining accommodations until the rest of the situation is resolved, after which everybody can go home."

"Fine then," I say, sitting next to Dolly. Everybody finds chairs, the additional personnel shuffling in as Will sits on the other side of me. On impulse, I take his hand briefly, squeeze it, and smile when he looks at me.

Papers are passed out to each of us, depositions practically, and I do in fact take the time to read the entire thing. Bits did as well. Marquis. Dolly, however, only takes out her e cigarette, and gestures with it as if to say "this alright?" When nobody stops her, a sweet cherry pie smell lightly puffs through the room.

"You're not reading it? You trust your compatriots that much?" Mr. Harding asks.

"I do," Dolly says, and blows a smoke ring. "Haven't led me wrong yet."

None of the information about the stolen stones references anything about hidden data, or indicates in any way that they're more than just diamonds. Bits and I glance at each other, and I raise my eyebrows just slightly. Bits blinks once, slowly. She has copies.

"Problem, ladies?" Mr. Harding asks from his seat at the head of the table. None of the other staff have spoken, and I wonder what sort of deals this room has witnessed.

"There is the question of delivery," I say.

"Pardon?" Everybody in the room looks up.

I plant my finger on the applicable line. "It says here that upon signing, we will deliver the missing package in full. As stated, we are not currently in possession of the package. It's in a secure location. However, that location will be burned for us immediately should we subsequently be chauffeured in SU-Vs and black helicopters and whatnot for your recovery's sake. That is not acceptable to our business model."

"You'll notice we do not really indicate the illegality of your business model or the means by which you came by the package," Mr. Harding says. "We could make those adjustments as well if you'd like."

"And nullify our agreement in its entirety, as it predicated upon the amnesty and the payment these documents also indicate." I smile.

"That's why I let them read it," Dolly says to the room at large.

"Disappointingly, my documents discuss no packages, so I feel safe signing them. Unless as a show of solidarity I ought not?" Marquis asks, and I feel wildly relieved. They aren't so mad at me that we won't move past it.

"No, darling, go right ahead if you feel like you're all set. Our agreements shouldn't affect one another's."

"They are entirely separate," Harding says, and one of the notaries nods. Mr. Harding continues to study me, and I do not waver. "It says staff accompaniment, does not specify number of staff, or describe the vehicle type. It satisfies the agreement for Will to accompany you."

"I think that is a generous interpretation of the papers you have given us, Mr. Harding, and if that is the spirit of what this agreement is, I am more than happy to sign it."

"Is that okay with you too?" Mr. Harding turns to Bits.

"Yeah. Looks good." She shrugs, still reading, but doesn't bring up any other issues once she's finished.

"It's a good thing you all were so willing to be reasonable," Mr. Harding says. "Pens are there on the table, Marquis will receive payment and transportation immediately. Will is empowered to distribute payment once the package is in hand."

"Splendid," I say, but I use a pen from my purse. It isn't often that I hand write something, and I have a particular pen that I feel shows off my penmanship the best.

Chapter Fifteen

When they let us leave, three days later, we don't receive another submarine ride. Instead, we take an elevator for an interminable number of floors to the surface, and then up from there, wordless and off-rhythm muzak plaguing us for the duration.

//Can I hack it and change it?// Bits texts me.

I smile thinly and shake my head. //Best to keep some cards up our sleeve, just in case.//

"So I don't really get where the threat went," Dolly says.

"What do you mean?" Will asks.

"We fled here by cover of night and water, by the skin of our teeth near as I could tell. We could smell the cordite. And now in three days it's just kinda...done?"

"Our people have worked to confuse the signals they've been using to find you. The various satellite tags which identify you as you have been replicated hundreds of times across the city and increasingly beyond. It makes that method of search useless, unless they have unlimited personnel and resources."

"Not necessarily," Bits says as the elevator doors ding open and we escape our canned music hell. "The right algorithm could knock down the false positives in almost no time at all just by comparing the movements against the original sample.

Then they'd have a much narrower scope to search, and if each individual they had on it took a vector, they'd drop it even faster."

"So how much time are you saying we might conceivably have?" I ask.

Bits shrugs. "A couple hours. Or thirty minutes. It depends on the quality of their equipment and personnel. Or I could just be paranoid and everything will go according to plan."

"I am so fucking glad you said that," Dolly says, looking up at the sky.

"I knew you would be."

"Look, there are other reasons it's done now. Let's...let's just get in the chopper," Will says.

"To where?"

"Ladies' choice, I guess. To one of our motor pools, or back to your car."

"Our car is all right?" I ask.

"Last I knew it was. When the opposition swept in, they gave the vehicles a cursory search and scan, but they know what they're looking for, obviously, and how best it could be hidden."

"Well, they think they do," Bits says.

"Why you wicked girl, whatever do you mean?" I ask. "You didn't actually leave the diamonds in the car?"

"Well, no. But you'll see."

"Well I know the suspense is killing me," Will says. "So have any of you ridden in a helicopter before?"

"Got my license to fly one," Dolly says.

"Really?" Will turns to stare.

"Dolly manages our vehicular needs," I say, gritting my teeth just a little. I'd previously mentioned a helicopter and she hadn't said a word. "And firearms, if such a thing becomes necessary."

"That detail had somehow escaped me," Will says. "The vehicle thing, not the firearms. Your car is so—"

"Unassuming? That's on purpose." Dolly shrugs. "Besides, it gets good mileage. Has one of the best and longest lasting batteries on the market."

"Especially with a little tweaking," Bits says. We settle our headsets and the rotors spin up. Dolly is not permitted to pilot.

A helicopter ride is interesting enough on its own, but we're over water for far longer than I anticipate, and I do get a teensy bit bored. I'd have preferred a night flight, with the city stretching out beneath us like jewels on velvet, dark buildings looming, encasing everybody's tiny lives within.

The shipyard does, in fact, look much as we left it. It was almost a disappointment, little sign of explosions or gunplay or our hasty exit, save for the fence in one area is a twisted ruin. The car is there, little dark sedan, just where we'd parked it. Windows intact, doors closed, trunk shut.

"I almost expected to never see the car again," I say once the helicopter is silent.

"It would've been a shame," Dolly says. "After all we put into it."

"I call shotgun," Bits says.

"I never get to sit up front," I say to Will.

"You never call shotgun," Dolly says, pressing her thumb to the lock until it beeps and unlatches all the doors.

"Excuse me, I didn't grow up 'calling shotgun.' And what's the other one you go on about?"

"Punch buggy," Dolly says.

"Punch buggy?" Will asks, eyebrows raised.

"VW Beetles? That they've made since the 20th? Apparently one exclaims punch buggy and punches the nearest passenger in the leg or arm."

"I'm really glad my brothers never knew that," Will says. "Not that there were many beetles where I'm from."

"There were like, three or four versions, but they kept making the original style in Mexico for decades after everybody else stopped." Dolly starts the car. "I'm not really sure why. But people would go south of the border and drive them up. Hell, they might still do it. And where I'm from, the weather's good for cars. So. Lots of punch buggies."

"Your childhood must have been amazing," I say dryly.

"Got real good at not hitting like a girl," Dolly says. "Because my brothers're the ones who taught me."

"What about you, Bits? Any punch buggying in your household?" Will asks. Bits has the VR headset on, her head tipped back against the seat rest.

"We didn't have many road trips," she says distantly. "And I don't have any brothers. Lots of cousins. Turn right here."

"We came from—" Will starts, and I lay a hand on his arm.

"Just let them." From the way his suit moves, and the slight crackle, the inner right pocket is where he has our documents. I envision manila envelopes, one for each of us, each containing a passport and a pay chip and a copy of our amnesty agreements.

"You don't know either?"

"I was out with you, remember?"

We drive for twenty or more minutes, then pull into a bus station that looks like it hasn't been used since the original bugs were rolling off the line. Grass grows up through the cracks in the pavement, and the perimeter fence has sagged into a metal haystack in the weeds, as though the big bad wolf huffed and puffed and blew the house down.

"We're clear," Bits says, and Dolly parks just around the back and cuts the engine.

"I don't get it," Will says. "Why an abandoned bus station?"

"Well. This isn't a hangout. It isn't along a well traveled road. There may or may not be some serial killer rabid dog bogeyman kinds of stories about this bus station in particular."

Dolly muscles open the half unhinged door, which to my eye seems as though it was last opened before any of us were born. It's bright inside, not like a closed building at all, and when we step through the opening, we look up at the clear blue sky through a tremendous hole in the roof.

"Everybody's up on their tetanus shots, right?" Dolly asks.

"Actually, yes," I say. It only seems prudent.

"Yup," Bits says.

"It's regulation," Will says.

Dolly laughs. "Geeze, folks, I was mostly jokin'. But it's good to know we're all covered." Bits keeps her headset on, but every once in a while lifts it and peers around at the real world.

"I never would've guessed you were into urban exploration," I say, picking my way through the broken tile, the roots which have heaved themselves up from the dirt below.

"It has its uses," Bits says.

We reach the wall of bus station lockers, which are improbably pristine, unbent, unrusted, and most of them with their keys still inserted. Dolly catches my eye, then grins and winks before producing a key, orange plastic fobbed, from one of her many, many vest pockets. Bits takes out a similar one and goes to a locker near the middle, surrounded by other doors missing keys. Dolly goes to a locker near the end, near the women's room, the big long sign hanging off of one rusting, weeping bolt. Each pull out a green enameled, workman's style thermos.

I rummage in my purse for a lipstick to apply while watching the proceedings. "That was dreadfully clever. Is that all of them?"

"Yup," Bits says.

I turn to Will, smiling. "Isn't it grand?" I ask, and I step in towards him. Reflexively, he puts his arms out, and I put my hands on his lapels, stand on tiptoe, and kiss him full on the mouth, lightly at first, but then he closes the circle of his arms around me, and we lean in together for a blissful moment.

He breaks the connection first, moving as though he stumbled while taking a step, but we're both standing still. I slip a hand inside of his suit coat, pull out the envelopes. "Wha—" he starts, and then his voice fails him. Dolly and I guide him to sit in one of the bolted-in bus station chairs that remains.

"I'm sorry, Will, I know you intended to keep your end of the bargain. We simply couldn't trust Mr. Harding and the rest of them, though." I raise my eyebrows at Bits, who opens the thermoses and selects a couple of the black velvet bags, dropping them into one of those silvery signal-blocking bags she keeps on hand. "These are the dangerous ones," I say. "The ones with nasty locations, and launch codes, and all that Dead Hand business. These others, while very interesting, contain no threat to anybody. They're simply too lucrative to let go. You do understand, don't you?" He just looks at me mutely, betrayal writ large in his brown eyes. I pat him on the cheek as he tries to speak again. "I haven't killed you, if that's what you're worried about. Either your compatriots will find you, or you'll recover and be able to call them."

"We done here?" Dolly asks.

I take out my last handkerchief, carefully blot off all my lipstick. "I should think so."

"Whenever we get used to a place..." Bits says as we walk out to the car, headset hanging around her neck like flight goggles. "Time to move again, I guess."

Epilogue

Though I have never been religious, I always pause and turn my head in the proper direction when I hear the call to prayer waft through my silk-hung windows, borne on the sea breeze towards the stunning blue waves, the world beyond. It is deeply beautiful to me, and I respected it. Perhaps one day I shall convert to something, perhaps not.

There's a light rap on my door. "We've got some early birds," Suzette says. She's the first friend I've made here. She's from Paris, and she loves party nights as much as I do. My little apartment is much like the one I last had in America, without much in the way of furniture, but perfect to fill with people and drinks and hors d'ouevres.

"I'll be right out!" I return my attention to the cosmetics arrayed on the table in front of me. I've already put in my diamond earrings, hung a thin golden chain around my neck, the barest whisper of precious metal against my pale collarbones. The night promises to be clear, and while my hand hesitates on the Chanel, I pass it over for the sandalwood rose, spritzing my inner wrists, the hollow of my throat, the back of my neck. I apply my lipstick, blot, take a moment to look at myself in the mirror. I admire the speckled light reflected onto my skin from the Fabergé egg set there on a little pedestal, risen above the other bits and baubles. I draw a finger along the edge of it, for the pleasure of it, then stand.

I imagine Will is going to show up any day now, and it remains to be seen if it is with or without the cavalry. I switch off the light as I go to meet my guests, leaving the torn-open air mail envelope to fuss a little in the breeze, with its stamps upon stamps, forwarded and forwarded, until it reached me here on this foreign shore.

Jennifer R. Donohue grew up at the Jersey Shore and now lives in central New York with her husband and her Doberman. Though she got a bachelor's degree in psychology, she has always wanted to write. She currently works at her local public library, where she also facilitates a writing workshop. Her work has appeared in Daily Science Fiction, Mythic Delirum, Syntax & Salt, Escape Pod, and elsewhere. She blogs at Authorized Musings, where she shares fiction and the tribulations of the writing life, and tweets @AuthorizedMusin.

Preview

Run With the Hunted 2: Electric Boogaloo
Chapter One

There's a dead pixel in the sky. Once I notice it, I can't ignore it. My eyes keep dragging up to look, no matter where I am and what I'm doing. It's an itch I can't scratch, a smear on the lens of my immersion. Plus, I don't know how long it's been there.

The moon is always somewhere real-time appropriate. They tried the stars, in beta, but it took far too much bandwidth and nobody wanted a project like that. Now most places, it's flat black at night, sometimes cloudy. The moon. A comet, if one is visible to the naked human eye. It's ridiculous, what people bicker over when given the forum. Not a surprise. Just ridiculous.

So now that's my pet project. I spend my time adding stars. My personal night sky is a complete one, and when I have the time or the urge, and I've got a lot of time, I go through the old Hubble and Cassini and Kepler photographs and further enrich the night sky, so if I want to spend time virtually lying on my back on a mountain or rooftop, just looking at all of the stars mankind had ever heard of, I can do that. I upload it to the public servers, little by little. My VR immersion rig is the best one money can buy, but the others are catching up. Managing the data better, with solid states and local nodes and the new fiber infrastructures.

I sometimes going to Carnivale in Venice at nighttime, the only place you can visit Venice anymore, the crenellated buildings all scanned and then rendered true to life, buildings which aren't standing in Venice anymore, sucked into the mucky lagoon or swallowed up by the waves or what have you. The twinkle lights, the gondolas. Everybody there is always all dressed up and masked. It adds another dimension, more dimensions, the party plus the game of identifying human or program. It isn't as easy like it used to be, to tell if something, somebody, humanoid is a human in virtual reality, or an AI. On impulse, I stop a man in a giraffe mask and, through my unicorn mask, ask "Do you see that in the sky?"

He looks down at me, and then up at the night, shook his head. "See what?" he asks. He's human. I'm good at the Uncanny Valley game. I'm good at the Human or AI game. I'm not good at dealing with people in real life.

"Nevermind. Bug hunting." He nods and goes on his way. My nose itches and I wrinkle it distractedly. Next is to find somebody in the same VR node as me. Theoretically. Except my VR node is just mine, paid for in an isolated jungle in Mexico, my rig built by hand piece by piece and hooked up to the local fiber after greasing appropriate political palms up the ladder, through intermediaries. Intermediaries were much better than me doing it. This could be real bad. I move off the street, out of the crowd, and start my immersion exit protocol sequence to boot out of VR. It's been awhile, actually. Longer than a public protocol would've allowed. Public protocols existed for a reason, I'm happy to acknowledge that. But really they're unnecessary limits. Turns out, when you have the money for it, anything's possible.

The Carnivale around me fades away, the sounds and smells first, and the sights, like an old fashioned photograph un-developing, and I'm left temporarily with the flat gray haze of the nonwaking state. It's drug induced, meant to be a body-brain buffer between the shock of VR immersion and consciousness, or vice versa. It isn't necessary if you're just upright using a VR headset. It isn't necessary if you're still just living your life. Do I feel the needle sliding into my arm? It's public protocol, but not my protocol. I'm cotton-mouthed, not quite conscious, unable to protest.

After a moment, things come into sharper focus. The room's still dim, but ambient sounds return, the hum of servers and their water coolant, a compressor somewhere. Breathing, my own and somebody else's. The flat plastic smell of the carpet, still pretty new, mixed with the antiseptic smell of the medical equipment for VR immersion, the IV rig, all of that. The grass and gun oil smell of the intruder. I open my eyes slowly; eyelids tend to stick, especially after so long.

Dolly grins down at me. "Hey Bits," she says. "I wasn't sure tapping your machine with a hammer was the best way to wake you, but I guess it got the job done. Hope I shot you up with the right stuff once that light turned green."

"Oh Jesus Christ, Dolly, what're you doing here?" I ask hoarsely.